TIMBERLINE

A ROAMER WESTERN

TIMBERLINE

MATTHEW P. MAYO

FIVE STAR
A part of Gale, a Cengage Company

GALE
A Cengage Company

Farmington Hills, Mich • San Francisco • New York • Waterville, Maine
Meriden, Conn • Mason, Ohio • Chicago

LIBRARY OF CONGRESS CATALOGING-IN-PUBLICATION DATA

Names: Mayo, Matthew P., author.
Title: Timberline / Matthew P. Mayo.
Description: First edition. | Waterville, Maine : Five Star, a part of Gale Cengage Learning, 2018. | Series: A Roamer Western
Identifiers: LCCN 2017053608 (print) | LCCN 2017057309 (ebook) | ISBN 9781432842864 (ebook) | ISBN 9781432842857 (ebook) | ISBN 9781432842840 (hardcover)
Subjects: | BISAC: FICTION / Action & Adventure. | FICTION / Westerns. | GSAFD: Western stories.
Classification: LCC PS3613.A963 (ebook) | LCC PS3613.A963 T56 2018 (print) | DDC 813/.6—dc23
LC record available at https://lccn.loc.gov/2017053608

First Edition. First Printing: May 2018
Find us on Facebook–https://www.facebook.com/FiveStarCengage
Visit our website–http://www.gale.cengage.com/fivestar/
Contact Five Star™ Publishing at FiveStar@cengage.com

Printed in the United States of America
1 2 3 4 5 6 7 22 21 20 19 18

To Jen and Tess . . .
Oh, lucky, lucky me!

"The Devil pulls the strings which make us dance;
We find delight in the most loathsome things;
Some furtherance of Hell each new day brings,
And yet we feel no horror in that rank advance."
—Charles Baudelaire

CHAPTER ONE

I never expected to see a monkey that morning at the Williwaw train station. It being the middle of October made the discovery all the odder. Seems to me monkeys shouldn't be in the fickle climate of northern Oregon. They should be in tropical places, enjoying fruit and squabbling with other monkeys high up in the treetops. Of course, none of this stopped me and the dozen or so other folks waiting on the rain-sogged loading platform from staring at the little creature.

The monkey's hide was dark brown at the tips, lighter beneath, and sort of tufty where it stuck out around his red coat. He—that's my assumption, though I didn't get close enough to verify—was no bigger than a barn cat, but with little, delicate hands that gestured and reached as a person might. I reckon we are closer to the animal world than the Bible whackers care to admit. What is it they're afraid of, anyway?

That monkey didn't seem to mind the miserable gloomy weather, the bite in the air that carried the promise of snow. Maybe it was the attention he was getting from all those people. I was grateful to the little fella, who kept everyone's stares from me and my big, hard-looking face. I am what the less-kind folks among us call ugly. That's the plain truth of it. I know it and I can't do a thing about it. I shave and I look worse. I don't shave and I look like a bear in man's clothing who decided to step out and wander on down from the mountains and into town for supplies.

I've been called everything from homely beast to killer and thief, all unwarranted, I hasten to add. And though I usually elicit little more than sharp-drawn breaths, tight-set teeth, and wary glances as people hustle by me, occasionally I will hear a stifled gasp and know it's nothing more than a reaction to my appearance. This sort of reception only reaffirms my natural inclination to spend as much time apart from civilization as I can. That, in turn, has led to me earning names I don't mind, closer as they are to the truth.

Nomad, vagabond, wanderer, drifter, I've been called them all. The only one that stuck is "Roamer," given to me by my friend Maple Jack, the crusty old mountain man I consider my mentor. He considers me a burr under his saddle blanket.

Sometimes I call him my tormentor. He's a mountain man and a whole lot more. Mostly he's a raconteur of the highest order. I told him that once, knowing full well he is aware of the meaning of the word.

He fixed a lone, hairy eye on me, piercing through the spidery shrubbery of his facial hair and eyebrows. "You call me that again, whelp, and I'll have no choice but to take a round or two out of you. And don't think I can't!" He then wagged a thick finger at me.

I recall not suppressing a bark of laughter. He winked and turned back to stirring that godawful-smelling stew he'd been building for half an hour. I don't know what he puts in his stews when my back is turned, but it's usually something un-toothsome, concocted so he'll get the lion's share of the foul, bubbling meal. Fine by me.

I'd laughed at his threat, but the truth is, Jack's a powerful fellow with more grit and scrap in him than any I have ever met. I hope I'm not too far down that list myself. I'm well north of six foot, big at the shoulder, and I don't carry much reserve flesh, as Jack refers to his paunch.

If I had a say-so, I'd not have been born looking the way I do. Scorfano is the name given me by the people who birthed me, then gave me up to be raised as a laborer on their plantation. I ran away when I was but a lad and, until I met Jack, fended for myself. That I'm still alive is a testament to the power of good fortune, and reliance on instinct. Scorfano means "ugly one" in Italian. On that score I will agree with them. I was born homely and that hasn't changed in the intervening years. In fact, it's only gotten worse because I've taken a few knocks that have not improved my looks.

All that said, I am no hermit, and I do enjoy the company of others on occasion. And yet, whenever I do venture into a town, mainly to restock my meager required supplies—coffee beans, cornmeal, flour, salt, dried beans, canned fruits in syrup, waxed thread for repairs, needles for said thread, and a small stack of other useful items—I am reminded why I should have stayed away. I've been beaten, stabbed, jailed, and clubbed in the head more times than I care to recall. Or maybe it's more times than I can recall, which is much closer to the truth, I suspect, given how tender a man's bean can be. Even my shaggy head.

The fellow tending the monkey, possibly a Basque from the looks of his jaunty beret, stroked the monkey's cheek, smiling in fondness. The monkey, unlike so many kept creatures exploited for financial benefit, appeared happy with his lot and accepted a peanut from the man's grimy, work-creased hand.

A young woman at the front of the tiny crowd raised her head and asked the Basque a question. "May I . . . that is, does he bite?"

The man smiled and shook his head. "No, no, it's okay! He will not bite, not bite." He nodded at her, encouraging her.

She reached a tentative gloved hand, soft blue kid leather, toward the monkey, palm up. The monkey set his own slender hand right in hers as if they were about to shake. Wonder of wonders. Like a little person, he was.

I watched the young woman's profile as she turned, smiling. Right then, I felt a stab, like a hatpin had slid between my ribs and deep into my heart. She looked to be perhaps twenty years old. A lock of wispy blond hair hung over her face, loosed from beneath a hooded wool cloak of a blue I've only seen on flowers on fine painted porcelain.

Her skin's pallor resembled the rest of that porcelain—white, but with the faintest bloom of pink riding high on her cheeks. Her chin was prominent and bore a slight cleft in the center. Faint purple smudges rested beneath her bright, wide eyes, a blue nearly as rich as that of her cloak, and wreathed by long lashes. She looked to be a young woman getting over a sickness that had somehow enhanced her beauty. At least that's the fanciful line of thought I caught myself trailing. I averted my gaze as she turned and made her way through the little crowd, which parted before her as if she were a magical being.

She was smiling and talking to an old woman who I now saw held the young woman's elbow in a firm grip.

Great lummox that I am, so says Jack, I was neither fleet enough of mind nor foot to turn away before she reached me.

". . . a homely thing," said the girl as she looked up at me, not but two or three inches from me. She wore a delighted look conjured by the monkey. I could have bent down and kissed her, so pretty and startled did she seem. But her comment settled like a scrim of soot on the moment.

She looked into my eyes and her mirth was replaced with the inevitable fear and pity. Revulsion would be next. I turned from her gaze even as the old woman scowled at me and jerked the girl's arm, guiding her away from this brute who had ruined their moment of happiness.

Not for the last time that day, nor the first time in my life, did I chide myself for indulging in thoughts that would never lead to anything but grief. Why, I wondered, had I indulged in my foolish notion of giving myself a train trip? Was the satchel of new-to-me books not enough? No, apparently not. My ill-suited reasoning had begun months before.

Every year and a half or so, for the past several years, I have altered my usual unplanned rambling lifestyle to take on cash-paying work. As my needs for goods offered by others are few, I find I am able to make the money I earn last a good, long while. In late August I hired on as a teamster for the Sovereign Star freighting outfit. It promised to be the short-term work that suits me.

I don't mind spending hour after hour on the trail, alone in a laden wagon, the oxen grinding away slowly before me, their steady steps as predictable as the arms on a decent pocket watch. I often find teamster work when I need to refill my coin purse. I get hired because I know how to handle a team; I can lug freight, and load and unload wagons; and I tie down a load like no one you've ever seen. The secret is to keep the rope tight, and then tie a good many knots until you run out of rope.

But the real reason I get hired on, I know, is that I'm big and ornery-looking. Outfit owners doubt anyone will risk tangling with me on the trail, and in that they are so far correct. They also figure they'll save money by not hiring a shotgun rider, which also means there's no second driver to spell me. I don't mind such an arrangement, I find my own company is sufficient.

I hired on in Dulse, Utah, at Sovereign Star's headquarters, which sounds grander than it is. The business consists of a half-dozen wagons, a couple dozen oxen, a handful of mules, and Hester Dooley, the owner. She's also the widow of—and I quote Hester—"That fool of a man, Seamus, who stuck me with this godawful business. Useless as tits on a bull, he was . . ."

Hester is not a woman to suffer fools, but is generous with

wages. I concluded I would work for her again should the opportunity arise. In two months with the outfit, I worked my way northwestward into northern Nevada, through Oregon, and even into southern Washington, hauling supplies to farming communities, mountain mine camps, and a handful of trading posts. I hauled out furs, seed, grains, hay, and ore. It was interesting work. As I didn't have an armed escort, the prospect of danger kept me tight and wary.

My last run brought me to Williwaw, in northeastern Oregon. I'd arranged with Maple Jack months before that I would take the train from wherever my final run landed me, and meet up with him on or around October 14 in Deerhoof, Montana, at the depot of the Northern Overland High Line.

Jack would have Tiny Boy, my Percheron stallion, with him. A finer friend on the trail a man could not ask for. Tiny, who is anything but, rarely talks and appears to be of the ruminative sort, much the same as myself. I verified this because we can spend hours roaming the backcountry anywhere, each lost in our own reverie, and yet we move apace together, each guiding the other without thought. That is how I regard the relationship. Tiny, I am certain, takes a more practical view. He knows I carry apples and lump sugar.

From there, the plan was up to Jack, a point I'm not a little worried about. He's reluctant to share his notions with me, but when I proposed this idea to him back in August, he began to snarl and spout about how much work it was going to be for him: "Not for you," he'd said, "but for me and me alone!" The old, oddly healed pointer finger on his left hand, crooked and wagging in the air, punctuated his state of high dudgeon.

I'll admit it was a bit of selfishness on my part, but I also knew Jack had been planning on heading in roughly that direction anyway sometime in autumn. He wanted to flank the Bitterroot Range and work his way north before early mountain snows made travel too much like work. He was set to snail his way northwestward toward Salish Lake to spend the winter in relative warmth with his "winter woman," a frightening Salish woman who has buried more husbands than any woman I know. Jack is a man who gets downright gleeful when the odds in life pile up as imposing as a range of spiny peaks.

That all worked for me, as we both knew I'd feel that urge to roam, and within days, maybe a week, I'd depart from the tribe's camp and seek silence, and less companionship, elsewhere.

So that's what brought me to the train depot at Williwaw, Oregon, waiting on that gray-sky morning, a tang in the air tinkling warning bells in the back of my mind. I hefted the smaller sack, my war bag, holding my clothes, toiletries, and a handful of other items, including extra rations of jerky in case I found myself peckish and no meal forthcoming.

I hate to be hungry. Even more than that, I hate to not have tasty coffee at hand soon after I rise. A man can put up with a whole lot of discomfort and oddness in life, but the lack of bracing and hot coffee of a morning is, well, wrong.

In my other hand I held the leather handles of a large carpetbag, ratted around the corners, but bought used to haul the books I found in my teamster travels. This would be my only real indulgence in spending my hard-earned pay, but as vital to me as coffee. All told, I had enough good new reading to last me months, if I rationed myself.

It was a sizable haul, especially for someone who likes to keep on the move. But I figured I could stash them at Jack's place, swap books now and again, sort of like my own library. Oh, I know Jack will kick up a fuss, claim I'm abusing our relationship, that I'm taking advantage of a poorly old man. But we both know the truth. He's full of beans. And besides, the rascal likes reading as much as I do.

The only other thing in the bag with the books was a new

pair of bright red wool socks for Jack, a gift I felt certain he would like, even though he would yowl and carry on as if I had stuck him in the eye with a fishhook. Couldn't wait to give them to him!

CHAPTER TWO

I swore I wasn't going to let it happen—I swore before I hoisted myself aboard this rattling, rolling, grinding, squawking, smoke-blowing beast that I wasn't going to fall asleep. But I did. Something about trains never lets me keep my lids up and my brain alert. I don't need the opinion of a medical man to know it has something to do with the lulling sway and the steady clack-tickety-clack of the great brute as we snake our way along the tracks.

Despite my moaning, I do love riding trains. I believe I could ride a train half the days of each month and not tire of the journey. Any more than that, I fear the fun of it would wear down, like eating too many hot-from-the-oven biscuits with butter all at once. No matter how excellent they taste—and there is little in the world to rival the lofty wonder of a steaming biscuit, except maybe another one—you can overdo it. Trust me. I have tested this theory and come close to ruining that heaven-sent experience for myself.

The annoying thing about falling asleep on that particular stretch of the journey, I judged we'd not left the station at Williwaw more than an hour before, was the fact that someone had tugged down my furled brocade curtain, darkening my double seat at the far end of the car. That bothered me. I am usually more alert. Someone had had to reach over me to tug down that curtain and I didn't even wake up. So what woke me?

Then I heard it, a man's voice, low and rumbly. Then another, and maybe one more. Talking low, but not trying to be quiet, not caring who heard them. Through the windows across the aisle, I saw thick snow swirling. I prairie-dogged my head up above the seat—I'd been snoozing slumped, my head low, hat tugged down. I nudged the brim up and peered down the length of the car toward the far end, before the door that led to the caboose. I saw the source of the mumbly voices. Three men, one of them barked a laugh and I saw folks flinch, including the pretty young woman in the blue cape.

I sighed to myself. Why is the world riddled with inconsiderate jackasses? In my travels I've come across too many boors who feel they can do what they want when they want, no thought for anyone else. They are all tiresome, and never catch on that no one likes them.

As if to verify my suspicions, the man who laughed pushed up out of his seat, swaying more than necessary, even with the steady side-to-side motion of the rolling train. His face was puffy with sparse black chin hairs and a walrus moustache beneath a nose that resembled a crooked finger, accusing whoever he looked at of misdeeds only he suspected. He wore a short-waisted black wool coat, parted at the buttons. Redness showed in his eyes. He'd likely been drinking.

His two companions watched, one of them a squat-looking runt with a wet, pooched bottom lip, as if he were thinking of buying something but not yet convinced of its worth. His tongue darted in and out, a nasty pink snake inspecting the air. He wore a fawn-colored duster, buttoned tight to his neck, and a roll of jowl spilled out over the top. His ginger eyebrows had a spidery look to them. He was hatless and his head was nearly hair free atop, though the sides sported more of the same spidery hair, long and frizzed, as if he had been caught unawares in a summer electrical storm.

The third man, in shadow, sat erect. He wore a bowler atop

his head and a starched collar below his chin. Something about him spoke of money, or of someone who wanted to give that impression. Might have been the fresh haircut, the even, pink ears, the fact that he sat up straight, moving only slightly with the sway of the train. He wore a suit, dark in color, and the white of the collar formed a bright slope above the coat. His hair was sandy brown, and perched atop his head that bowler rode level-brimmed, as if balanced. I expect he was what most women might call dashing.

The swarthy drinker made his way toward the young woman, eyes fixed on her. Here comes trouble, I thought. And sure enough . . .

"Hey, hey, pretty lady." He stood over her seat, leaning, swaying in counterpoint to the car's motion.

She did not respond, but stared across at the old woman who accompanied her.

"Hey," he said, leaning down toward her, but still talking in his big manly voice. "You got no call to ignore me, see? Hector don't like to be ignored."

Still, she stared at her companion. Suddenly the old woman jerked her head up, her words lashing out like the spiked tip of a Mexican bullwhip. "See here, you uncouth brute—go away and leave us alone. You have no—"

He leaned down then, baring stained teeth behind pulled-back lips bristling with those sparse hairs. "You shut up, old cow. I was not talking to you. No man would talk to you, I bet." He brayed at his comment, then shot a glance at his two amused friends down the aisle.

His accent was difficult to place, and thick with drink, to boot. Perhaps he was Spanish, possibly Italian. I knew a smattering of words in each, but it didn't matter since he was rambling in English.

The old woman's eyes widened and her head snapped back

as if she'd been smacked. I could almost hear her whisper, "I never . . ."

The girl scooted toward the window in an effort to get away from the man. Hector took that as an invitation and slid into the seat beside her.

I pushed up out of my own seat. It was enough to still any movement in the car. All eyes, those of the annoying threesome and the rest of the six or so cowed passengers as well, stared at me. My head came close to the ceiling, and I'm more than wide enough to fill the aisle. Thankfully my voice matches my build.

"That's enough, fella." I added a touch of growl to it.

I'll do anything to avoid a set-to. But as a wise man once told me (yep, Maple Jack again, wisest man I know, but don't tell him I said so, I'll never hear the end of it), "Don't go starting a fight, but make damn sure you're the one who finishes it."

Hector swung his bloodshot eyes upward. "You talking to me?"

I angled my way up the aisle, nodding. "Yep," I said, my hands resting on my sides, elbows out. "Yep, I reckon I am."

He looked up at me and swallowed, making a gulping sound.

A couple of seconds passed, no one said anything; then one of his compadres broke the spell. A Southern drawl said, "Please don't pay Hector any mind. He's had a few drinks, nothing more. I am sure the young lady will understand."

I turned toward the voice, peering at the far end of the car. The man in the bowler had spoken. His voice matched his look—arched eyebrow, almost a smirk on his mouth. I was about to ask if he was talking to me, but realized it would parrot the fool cowering beneath me.

I turned my attention back to Hector in time to see his right hand crawl beneath his open wool coat. He was fixing to do something that might result in pain to my person. I grabbed with my right hand beneath his chin, snagging a handful of coat and shirt and, judging from the man's howls, what must have been chest hair and skin. With my left hand I pinched his hand at the wrist, felt bones bend, something popped. He howled again.

I lifted him, saw a small dark shape fall from his hand and clunk to the seat—a derringer, I think—and hoisted the flailing fool, knocking his head on the paneled ceiling. Once, twice, and a third time. He groaned, I grinned. I blame the erratic movement of the train for those extra lumps he'd feel later.

I found his belt buckle with my left hand as I walked him, still fighting but with less vigor, back to his friends. Before I dropped him in his seat, I held him aloft once more with my right hand. He tried to rake my face with his grimy good hand. I swatted it away with my left and drove a quick, tight punch to that crooked nose. It bent and bled, as they always do.

By then his shirts had untucked and the knuckles of my right hand worked a solid set of dents into the underside of his grinding jaw and greasy chin.

It took two seconds to find the solid heft of his sidearm. I shucked it, a revolver, and stuffed it into my coat pocket. I detected no other obvious weapons and hoped that would do for the time being. It took both hands to give Hector a proper toss backward into his former seat. But I managed it—and kept my grin in place, too.

He landed with a wheeze and a crack. Like so many of his kind, he was a weak-kneed child at heart. He slumped, quivering, blood dribbling down his shirtfront. The shadow-filled car was silent for a moment. Daylight had begun to lose its fight with dark. More groans bubbled up from Hector.

Fancy Collar opened his mouth to speak and I leaned close, a thick finger held up before his face. "No sir, no more. You keep that fool quiet the rest of this trip, leave these poor ladies and the rest of the passengers alone."

"Or . . . ?"

I stared down at him, my nostrils flexing wide. It was all I could do not to use both hands on his smug, well-tended face. I fancy I smelled lavender wafting off the bastard. "You don't want to know, fella."

To my surprise, his eyebrows dipped down to a normal height and he offered the barest of nods, as if we had come to an agreement. I let it go, hoping the entire walk back down the car that none of them was spineless enough to be a backshooter.

I'd give that jackass Hector his pistol when the trip reached its end.

With the fun over for the time being, the car quieted and the passengers, reading, dozing, or gazing out the windows, seemed content to sway in their seats with the train's clacking rhythm. Cold crept in with the day's fading light. I hunched beneath my fleece-lined, green-and-gray wool mackinaw, and nudged my window's curtain aside.

Swirls of snow crystals, on the verge of deciding how big and bold and dangerous they wanted to grow up to be, pelted at the window. I'd prefer they stayed small and died in their cribs. That earlier scent I'd ignored back on the loading platform had been the cold, thin smell of coming snow. And now we were in it.

As I watched, gouts of black smoke from the chugging engine whipped and spun in a mad dance with the wind-churned snow.

I ran a hand up and down my face, feeling the oft-broken nose, the wide cheeks, the stubbly beard—I could shave twice a day, it seems, and not make much of an alteration in the forested features of my face. I tamped down a yawn, stretching my arms until my left shoulder offered up its customary pop and snap, a daily reminder of a fight I'd lost with a tree. But as Jack says, that's a story for another day. With everything back into place, I sat up straight in the bench seat and got a better look at my fellow passengers.

Most of the folks who'd been gathered around the Basque and his little monkey were now in the train's one passenger car. At the far end, toward the engine, the three men, the only ones among us I did not recognize from the platform, flanked the door, two on the left side, one on the right. None of them smiled. The train surged ahead, then slowed but kept moving. I peered again out the window. The day was headed quickly toward an early nightfall. The storm might well be a ripsnorter to grow dark that soon.

The three men, near as I could tell, were late arrivals. I'd seen the others of our small group climb aboard and take their seats, but somehow I'd missed these three. Had I really dozed off that quickly? I had, though for good reason. After leaving the employ of Hester Dooley's freighting outfit, I'd pushed hard to get to the station before the train departed, and made it with a couple of hours to spare.

Closer toward my seat, the rest of the passengers swayed and leaned on each other, against the windows, huddled in their frock coats and winter wear. One thin fellow with the look of a young, dandified barrister huddled in a light gray wool suit with black piping holding it all in. He looked particularly cold. I surmised he was caught unawares by the weather, probably more used to warmer southerly climes.

There was an older, portly man seated alone, like myself. He wore a high collar on a long gray wool overcoat. The collar was an odd-looking affair, but I bet it kept his thick neck warm. I have about the same height on my collar, and it does the trick on the trail when you need to bury your face out of the wind. He appeared to be deep in slumber. His fleshy cheeks wagged to the comforting rhythm of the train.

Across the aisle from him sat a chesty, plump woman wearing a deep-brim calico bonnet cinched tight around her face. She had an arm draped around the shoulders of a dark-haired boy who looked to be no older than eight years. He was of dark complexion and with wide eyes, maybe a Mexican boy. He seemed to be taking in everything around him.

His eyes caught mine and I smiled and nodded. He didn't look away, didn't appear startled, didn't smile, but continued staring at me. After a few moments, I got the impression he had satisfied himself. He looked back toward the window at the rushing wisps of smoke and snow.

Then I saw her, the girl in the blue hood. Only now she wasn't wearing it. It lay crumpled, pushed back off golden hair that shone even in the dim innards of the train car. She, too, was asleep. In a relaxed pose she was even prettier than when awake, if that were possible.

Seated across from her was the same older woman who'd guided her by the elbow back on the platform. Her silvered hair was pulled back tight and gathered in a pinned-up, fist-size bun on the back of her head, honeycomb lace wrapping it, as if to help minimize the severe look. It didn't work.

Ah well, I am forever accounting details in my head of strangers I meet, their clothes, hair and eyes, how they talk, kindly or otherwise. I expect it's an odd trait, but it has served me well in the past in avoiding trouble.

Train cars always look so handsome from a distance. Even up close, they're impressive. Then you climb inside and you sit on the leather seat waiting for the beast to grind and chug. You get to surveying the details of the woodwork and steel around you, and that's when you see signs of wood rot, the chipped paint, worn seats, threads and straw filling and wood stays poking through.

You see the smudged, sooty glass of the windows, the broken sash clasps. You smell the stale stink of coal and woodsmoke from a thousand fires in the little warming stove in the car's center. You hear the near-constant chitter of off-key squeaks and clicks as if trapped squirrels were plotting a breakout that never happens.

And I love every worn bit of it. As I said, I like trains. But I was beginning to suspect that I might whistle a different tune after this trip. It was becoming a tiny trial with signs of collapsing into a big one.

I glanced once more out my window and sighed quietly. This snowstorm would not be good for the train or the journey, especially headed into the mountainous terrain of the southern Bitterroots.

I rose to stand once more. A few folks turned their heads. I intended to stretch my legs, and determined to not look at the girl in the blue cape. No good can come of ogling such a fair creature. Mostly I had to stretch my pins—sitting too long is a painful endeavor.

I had it in my head to visit the caboose, where my bag of books resided. Some men nurture their guns above all else, polishing and rubbing and bluing. I agree it's important to keep one's tools in top condition, and I do maintain my Schofield to the best of my abilities. But I value my books, which are tools for my mind, more than other bits of my gear, the revolver included.

That said, I don't like to be without my Green River sheath knife, which always rides on my waist. It was a gift from Maple Jack some years back after he found I carried only a folding knife. "That tiny metal sliver," as Jack called it, "won't do more than get you killed should you rely on it in a survival situation."

I disagreed then and I still do. I'd rather have a small folding knife on me than no knife at all. But I wasn't about to let him in on that notion. When he gets contradicted, Maple Jack is one surly ol' mountain goat. He can slide into a full-bore pout that lasts for a week.

I walked toward the far end of the car once more. I never have been put off by a clot of sneering men who set their hats at intimidating angles. It's possible over the years I've become too harsh a judge of people before I get to know them, but I have experienced time and again that people will let you down. They may not mean to, but they do. I reckon that makes me a bitter man. So be it. It also makes me a guarded man. Except when I fall asleep and let people close my curtains . . .

I passed the pretty girl's seat again. I shouldn't have looked, but I did. I sneaked a glance at her. It has been a long time since anyone or anything has seized my breath in my throat. Last time I recall that happening was a few years back when I woke to find a big ol' silvertip boar grizz chuffing and snapping his teeth in my face. I survived, but . . . that's a story for another time.

But this girl, she stoppered my breath in my gullet twice in the span of a few hours. I looked down as I angled past—I can't quite walk full-on down the narrow walkway between seats. She was awake now and looking at me through those eyes that were bluer than the pretty hooded cape. Then a voice cleared. Twice.

It broke the spell-gaze I fancied the girl had put on me. I couldn't help it. I looked, the old woman's eyes replaced the girl's. These weren't so kind, nor so blue. The old woman looked as though she wanted to say something, but I didn't stay. I raised a finger as if to touch my hat brim. The hat I'd left on my seat. Classy, Roamer.

The inside of a train car feels too much akin to the inside of a house, so I refrain, unless I'm snoozing, from keeping my topper on my pate. I did steal another glance at the girl, bold of me and not something I would usually do, but she was the prettiest woman I have ever seen. I should not have looked, for I saw the thing I've become accustomed to seeing on people's faces, particularly women's. I saw the creepings of fear. Any spell that might have been was only in my own homely, addled noggin, nothing more.

The entire moment devoured maybe five clicks of a clock's fast hand, though it felt like forever. I hoped my inflamed ears, cheeks, and neck were hidden by my coat's big collar, for I felt the shame of being a fool as I strode fast for the end of the car.

I passed the men, noting only the presence of a now-snoring Hector and the bowler-wearing Fancy Collar. The fat, spidery-haired bald man was missing. I wrestled with the door's catch for a couple of seconds before I saw I had been tugging it in the wrong direction. The metal grab handle was cold enough I wished I'd worn my gloves. Red paint slopped on long before was worn and smoothed where countless hands had grabbed at it over the years.

Sudden cold air whooshed at me as I eased myself onto the small catwalk at the end of the car. I angled myself sideways and closed the door so the other passengers wouldn't be too put off by the cold air. I faced a similar door on the caboose. I stood for a moment, blinking and trying to pull in a few lung-fuls of cold, crisp air not tainted with smoke from the engine.

Not perfect, but still better on the eyes than inside. The oil lamps on trains sting the eyes and dull the nose and throat, and soot up the air in the car. Once it's too dark outside to see, watery eyes are a constant ailment among train passengers.

The scene between the cars was much the same as within—snow driving every which way. To the north, at my right, I made out the forming shapes of spruce forest, dark against the com-ing night and darker still against the glowing, snowed landscape. I swear the straggling trees were shifting, dragging themselves closer to the tracks. Twilight does that to a man's eyes, a fun game if you have your mind. If not, what a hell that would be—chased by trees. I wonder, do they ever catch up to a madman?

The train, already struggling to progress eastward, clawed

slower still. We weren't on a grade, so it must have been snow accumulating ahead of us. This could be a long two-day journey. A train trek I was on several years before required all able-bodied passengers to climb down and wade through waist-deep snow every few miles to clear the cowcatcher of calf-size wads of sticky snow.

One shovel among us all, and socks on hands for mittens, that's mostly what I remember. That and wondering if my hands would ever warm again. But that's February in the high plains. I should have known better, but I'd been younger, greener, and dumber. All lethal afflictions in the West.

But now it was October and I wagered I'd make my trip without incident caused by fall's finicky weather. It would appear I'm a lousy gambler.

The outer handle on the caboose door dipped, slopping up and down twice, as if someone was trying to get out. Then all at once with a burst of grating steel, the door jerked inward and a man emerged out of the shadowy depths of the caboose. He was looking down at where he was about to step out onto the grating. As he tugged the door closed behind him, his shoulders hunching from the sudden cold, he looked up and saw me.

"What do you want? What are you doing here?" It was the bald, spider-haired fat man.

"Hi there," I said, holding up a hand. I jerked my chin upward. "Looking to get my bag from the storage car."

"That's no storage car."

"Well my belongings are in there."

"Not my problem," he said, eyes narrowing.

"What is your problem, then, fella? I aim to get my goods, and you aren't about to stop me."

"I . . . I work for the railroad, so you best shut your mouth, you hear?"

He sounded like someone who needed to be chucked off the

train. Every bit of me wanted to grab him by the throat and fling him into the snow. But between my dithering, being too kind for my own good, and the train slowing with each second, I didn't take my chance.

The man looked to his right, into the darkening night. "It's nearly time." He almost wheezed it out, so quietly did he say it, like a whisper.

"Time for what?" I said, annoyed that he broke off from our confabulation so easily.

He jerked his gaze back at me. "I told you to mind your own business."

"Technically," I said, wagging a big finger before his face, "you didn't say anything of the sort. You want to get your point across in life, fella, you're going to have to clean the gravel out of your mouth and speak your mind in full sentences and a clear voice."

"Why, you son of a—"

His right fist came up in a tight, quick arc. His follow-through was an abomination to everything pugilists hold dear. He missed me—I whipped my head to the side in time. His fist whistled past, sailing upward.

"You train for that?" I said, not hiding my grin. "Impressive."

He growled and lost his footing. His slick-soled boots slid on the steel platform. Down he went on one knee, groaning.

I figured if I gave him one more minute, he might do himself in, save me the trouble of dealing with his cantankerous hide. Meanwhile, a wintry gust blew the stink of engine smoke at us. It was bad enough that my opponent wobbled and coughed.

"What are you hiding in there, fella?" I asked.

Still kneeling, the bastard took another swing at me. Too much in too short a period.

"You know, fella," I said as he wheezed as if he'd run up and down a hill. "You ought not to be so high-strung. I only asked you a question."

The door through which I'd squeezed popped open and the well-shaved man, Fancy Collar, kicked his way outside. "What's going on here?"

"This big oaf tried to get by me, but I wouldn't let him."

"Why do you need to go in the caboose?" said Fancy Collar.

I narrowed my gaze. "I want something out of my bag." Truth be told, though I wanted to read, it was too late and too dark to get much reading in. Didn't matter, though. If they were going to play this way, so was I.

"Are you going to let me into that caboose or are we going to have a set-to right here, right now?"

"Aw, hell, Rufus, let him get his goods," said Fancy Collar. "It's not like we are hiding anything, right?"

But I saw the wink he gave fat, bald Rufus.

"Besides," he continued in that lazy Southern drawl. "As employees of the railroad, I reckon we have a sort of, um," he drummed his gloved fingertips on his gleaming chin, "obligation to treat our passengers kindly." He looked me up and down, his nose wrinkling theatrically as if he smelled a side of greening meat. "Even if they are . . ." his gaze settled on mine again, "different, shall we say."

"Mister," I said. "There isn't a thing you can say that will make me think any less of you. Now, my carpetbag."

Another look passed between the two men. I gathered Fancy Collar was the boss of the three-man crew. He was also not afraid of me. He kept eyeing me as if I were a curiosity, something unexpected but of potential use. That worried me. What were they up to? And what was so blamed important in the caboose?

I looked once more at the man before me in the doorway of that last car. He offered me his best deadly gaze. No doubt he considered himself champion of the skill and hoped to drop me

with it. I disappointed him. All it did was make me grin. "Step aside," I said, and he did, after getting a quick nod from Fancy Collar.

I pushed past him, trying to shut the door behind me, but he jammed a boot in the gap and forced it open again.

The warmth of the caboose was welcome. I walked to the little potbelly stove, my hands outstretched before me.

"That's my fire," said the man behind me.

"I don't believe a fire belongs to anyone. That's like laying claim to a stretch of river or an acre of ocean." I glanced at him, rubbing my chapped hands briskly over the stove's heat.

"Mister you talk a lot and don't say much."

I nodded, smiling, in no rush. "Heat enough for two but you ought to shut that door to capitalize on it properly."

Again the dumb stare. It became more obvious to me that the men Fancy Collar had surrounded himself with were not the sharpest knives on the rack. My suggestion leached into his addled bald pate and he stepped inside, shutting the door behind him.

I let my gaze drift over the contents of the car. Luggage was neatly stacked and stowed, various shapes of trunks, and a trousseau—I wondered if the fancy plaid-and-leather set belonged to the pretty girl and her matronly minder.

And there, from behind a homely stack of twine-wrapped packages, peeked my carpetbag. I did not buy it for its looks, but for its sturdy qualities. Any holes it has are made up for by the thick leather bottom, the oversize satchel handles, and the rawhide cinch and bone-toggle buttons.

I figured it would ride well enough behind the cantle on Tiny Boy's saddle. Not that he would care much—he's a Percheron, after all. Tiny is a big horse with a big attitude. Most of the time he doesn't much mind lugging weight. Sometimes he surprises me with a wild hair across his backside and then I have to keep an eye out for a quick flash of teeth. He might be sizable, but he can move like a rank-tempered barnyard goat when he gets an attitude. Which happens often enough.

I missed the horse and wondered if he missed me. Knowing Jack, he'd groused the entire time he took care of Tiny, all the while stuffing him with extra feed and snatches of that sweet-grass we'd labored to put in for the cold months the previous summer.

I reached for my bag and saw movement to my left.

"What are you doing?"

I let out a big sigh, weary beyond measure. "My bag, remember? The reason I paid you a visit here in your hidey-hole in the first place?"

I shoved the parcels out of the way and dragged my bag forward. As I did, I saw the unmistakable solid-steel corner of a safe, adorned with gilt filigree, like you'd see in a bank, only a little smaller. The sort you find on trains. Of course, trains always roll with payroll, cash, important paperwork, deeds, bonds, and the like. This train, apparently, was no different.

That might explain this joker and his two cohorts in the other car. And it gave more credence to Fancy Collar's claim about them being in the employ of the railroad. But three men? That had to be one cash-packed safe. It was also possible they were simply moving from one job to another and more-than-amply manned to keep an eye on the contents of the caboose.

A third option, one I didn't like, occurred to me. Might be none of them were railroad men. Not a shock given how uncouth they all seemed, even Fancy Collar, who tried too hard to exude the ways of a gentleman.

"Well, get on with it, then."

"You bet," I said, tugging the bag free. I balanced it on the edge of the wood-and-steel shelf while I unbuttoned, then unlaced and untied, the top. The mouth of the bag parted and

there were my books, jumbled despite my padding them with a ragged shirt.

The man, I noted, had sidled closer. I looked over at him and caught him angling for a look inside my bag. He saw me and rasped a hand across his pudgy chin. "What you got there?"

"Books," I said.

"Books?" It was as if the word itself were about to bite the inside of his mouth.

"Yep, books."

"What for?"

"To read. That's generally why folks have them."

His eyebrows pulled together into a squint. "Mister, that's about the craziest thing I ever heard."

I chuckled, fingered among the books, and tugged out a battered but intact copy of *The Count of Monte Cristo*.

"What's that one?" he said, bolder now that he'd determined I was crazy.

I told him the title, then said, "It's about a fella who's thrown in jail for the wrong reasons. But he escapes. Then the fun begins."

"You mean you already know what's gonna happen?"

"Yep, read it before."

He stared at me again as if I had eaten a live snake. "And you're fixing to give it another run. Hoo-boy! What people do with their time." He shook his head as if in disagreement. "I reckon I'd rather drink or find me some lady's company a whole lot more than I would sit and stare at all them little ants on those pages yonder." He nodded at the book I'd opened at random.

I closed it, tucked it under my arm, and fastened the bag shut again. "That's why the world is such a fascinating place, fella."

"How's that?"

"Takes all kinds to make it spin. Some folks are active, some passive."

"Don't know about that, but you darn sure are a bookish sort, even if you don't look much like one."

I was about to ask what a bookish sort resembled, but this conversation was chasing its tail, and I was losing prime, precious minutes for reading.

"That's it, then." I shoved the bag back into its little cubbyhole, did my best to ignore the poorly hidden face of the safe back there, and pawed the twine-tied bundles back into place.

I edged by him toward the door, reluctant to give up the fine heat thrown from that caboose. Now that would be a good spot for reading and dozing in quiet, warm comfort. I touched the book to my forehead in salute. "Obliged."

"Enjoy your book." He grinned and shook his head. I heard his cackle of laughter as I shut the door behind me. His loss, same thing I always think when I encounter mockery of the written word rearing its stunted, dull-eyed head.

What were these men about? I wondered as I paused between cars, eyeing the fading scene to my left, the north. Still we churned our way through the snow, which looked to be stacking up. I wondered if we would all soon be summoned to help clear the tracks.

I sighed once more—a habit I could do without. It makes me sound like a tired old man. I'll save that for when I really am one, if I make it that far. I opened the car's door and edged inside.

The passengers appeared the same up and down the length of the car, a few looked my way. I glanced down at the two men flanking me, Fancy Collar on one side, Hector still lolling in his seat on the other side of the aisle. Fancy Collar nodded at me. "I hope you found what you were so earnestly looking for."

In response, I held up the book, then edged on down the length of the car to my seat.

CHAPTER THREE

I was able to read the first dozen or so pages of Alexandre Dumas's classic novel before the light failed me. At that my eyes strained and I hugged the window, book angled to the light. The brightness of the snow helped. Along about that time, my head began to nod once more. As I faded into sleep, I had the barest awareness of the train struggling harder.

I woke some time later in near darkness, lit only with the erratic glow of a single oil lamp in the center of one wall of the car. The lamp swung with violence, whipping in an arc on its pivot. It swung because the train had slammed to a stop. We heard its great chesty roar exhaling with gusto, slow and certain, as if it were a dragon pondering its next move.

But this dragon shouldn't be sitting still. Something was wrong.

I pushed up out of the seat and was about to reach for the swinging lamp when the old woman did so.

"Everybody okay, then?" I said, scanning the car. They were in their seats, and from the looks on their faces, all were as cold and uncomfortable as I was, and had also been roused from sleep.

A few mumbles, some nods.

"What's happening?" said the skinny dandy.

"I don't know," I said. "You fellas have any thoughts?" I nodded toward the men at the end of the car, noting that the bald man had still not returned. Hector nodded as Fancy Collar spoke to him in a low whisper, both of them glancing at me, then looking back at each other.

"I said, do you fellas happen to know what's going on? You are employees of the line, after all. It's not likely we're scheduled to make a stop out here, is it?" I looked at the window, fruitless, as it was crusted with frost on the inside, and dark beyond. Maybe we were tanking up on water.

A fresh gust of wind slammed the train car, eliciting a flurry of gasps from the passengers.

"No," said Fancy Collar. "But since you're so curious . . . fella . . . why don't you toddle on up to the engine and find out, then come back here and let us know?"

We glared at each other for a few long moments. This was becoming tedious. "You know, that's a good idea," I said. "Why didn't I think of that? Might be because I am no railroad employee. If I were, my intellect would be honed to a razor-sharp edge and I expect answers to most of life's plaguing questions would trip from my tongue."

The pretty girl giggled, hid her mouth behind a gloved hand, and looked down. I could still see a slight smirk as she struggled to not look my way. I also saw the old woman's pointy boot nudge the girl on the leg. That settled her down.

Fancy Collar, too, had seen the girl's laugh, and his casual grin tightened into a sneer.

I turned back toward the front of the car and shoved open the door. I'd closed it behind me when a man covered in soot angled around the tender's catwalk, his eyes smarting and red-rimmed.

"What are you doing?" he said, eyeing me up and down with a squint.

"The passengers . . . we're wondering why we've stopped."

"Why you think?" The man shook his head and bit the ends of his gloves' fingers, tugging them off. "Me and Earl been

Matthew P. Mayo

fighting this weather for hours and it gets worse and worse." He looked past me at the closed door of the passenger car. "This route's usually off the books in the winter—tanks freeze. But the bosses thought we could squeeze in one more run before the weather turned." He sneered, his teeth bright against the soot-black of his face. "Like to see them out here now!"

He leaned against the black steel of the tender and knuckled an eye, grinding the soot deeper. "Since we're at the top of a grade, we're thinking we might be able to plow on through. But as this ain't our usual run, I don't much recall what the bottom will have in store for us. Wanted to let everyone know to set themselves for a jolt. Still early enough in the storm we should make it up the next grade. Didn't want you all worried. If we have our way, we ain't about to stop again unless we get bogged in a drift."

Even though we were the only two people in sight, he lowered his voice and leaned close. "Still," he scratched his stubbled, blackened chin, "supposed to be a short run, barely two days. But it ain't looking good. Don't go spreading that around, will you?"

"Don't worry," I said. "I'll tell the others to brace themselves. Might as well move forward while we can."

"That's what I was telling Earl. Much obliged." He turned back toward the engine once more. I touched his arm. "Say, you know those railroad fellas back there with us?"

"Who?"

"Three of them, end of the car. Claim they work for the railroad."

The man shook his head. "Uh-uh, mister. You been misinformed. Me and Earl and Benny, he's the conductor, of course, are the only employees on this train. On account of it being so small."

"Must be I misheard," I said, offering the man a smile. He

38

gave a tired salute and began tugging on his gloves as he walked back around to the engine.

Benny was the conductor. But where was he? I didn't want to ask the engineer because he'd get suspicious and go rooting around back there himself. That was a job I could do. But the dim, far-off tolling of a bell in the back of my brain warned me something about this trip had already derailed.

Logic told me Benny was either one of the three strange men, or he'd not remained aboard back in Williwaw, or he'd met with a mishap, likely caused by the strange men. I pushed my way back into the passenger car.

The rest of the passengers weren't pleased with my news, but most seemed to understand it was a kindness on the engineer's part to have told us.

"Ahem," said the dandy, standing and tugging on his vest as if he was about to speechify. And he was. "I for one have no desire to be involved in a wreck."

"A wreck?" said the fat woman seated across from him, clutching the quiet little Mexican boy close to her ample bosom. "Oh dear me, oh dear . . ." She was on the edge of a whopping sob, I could tell.

"Furthermore," said the dandy, waving a long, bony finger.

"Now, now," I said, holding up a hand. "Nobody said a thing about a wreck." I tried to keep my voice calm and casual, but it was difficult not to grit my teeth as I looked at the damnable dandy. "I expect the railroad's own employees, right here in our midst, can explain the situation better." I gestured toward the men at the end of the car.

Fancy Collar watched me a moment, then leaned back in his seat. "No, no, I reckon you've about covered it. There will be snow to plow through as we roll downslope, then with luck we'll gain the other side. Shouldn't be too long before we're on the flats again, wouldn't you say?"

I ignored him. Then I got an idea, not one of my brighter moments, in hindsight. But for good or ill, I always barge in on a situation and let the details emerge as I blunder ahead. I didn't stop at my seat but continued on toward the far end of the car.

"Whoa, whoa," said Fancy Collar, holding out a hand that stopped shy of grabbing my arm. "Where do you think you're going? Not to fetch another book, I hope."

"To see Benny," I said, resting my hand on the latch.

"Benny?"

"Yeah, you know . . . the conductor."

That pulled Fancy Collar up short. "Oh, Benny, yeah, he . . . he didn't stay on the train. He was needed elsewhere, said we could deal with any troubles that might arise, it being such a brief trip and all."

"So he's not in the caboose."

"That's what I said, Big Boy." Fancy Collar's tone during the entire exchange was steady and icy, like his eyes that never left my face. He was also speaking low. I was not.

"Here we go," said the dandy in a trembling voice as the train chuffed into motion.

The large woman moaned and squeezed that poor little boy to her bosom.

"Might want to take your seat." Fancy Collar smiled at me.

I dithered for a moment, on the edge of wanting to drop him low with a swift punch to his smarmy face. If ever a man begged for a fist, it was him. Not only because I suspected he was up to no good, but because he is handsome and he knows it. One of those fellas who can fall in an outhouse and climb out freshly laundered and smelling of lilacs and good times.

Instead, I kept my mouth shut, offered a slow nod, and returned to my seat—I'd heard what I needed to. I faced the rear of the train and kept Fancy Collar and Hector in my sights the entire time. I wasn't there for long.

CHAPTER FOUR

We pushed a whole lot of snow on our way down the grade. But there was something more belligerent than snow when we got to the bottom. Whatever we hit rattled the train, shook me in my seat, and slammed others into the laps of the folks seated across from them. This was a frightening prospect for the dandy, as he became wedged between the big woman's bosoms for a few smothering seconds. Once the train stopped, the shouts and wailing grew loud. But it was the not-so-muffled *ba-boom!* from the direction of the caboose that truly rattled everyone.

"What was that?" someone shouted.

Felt to me like an ill-timed attempt to blow the safe in the caboose.

About then, I noticed Fancy Collar was up. "Now, now, no need to alarm everyone but we're experiencing a few problems, I think it's obvious by now."

He strode up the aisle toward my end of the car. His compadre, Hector, also stood and slipped through the doorway to the caboose. Fancy Collar slicked out a Colt and cranked back on the hammer.

"Not so fast, Big Boy," he said as I reached for my Schofield. He shook his head and motioned for me to hand it to him.

"Like hell," I said, leaving my gun holstered but my hands poised.

He sighed and continued with his speechifying, keeping his eyes and his barrel's killing snout on me.

"As official detective on this railroad, I am in charge of your safety, ladies and gentlemen." Fancy Collar glanced around quickly, settling his eyes back on me once more, my hand twitching to snatch at the gun inside my coat. "Therefore, in the interest of safety, I am under strict orders to keep the peace." He looked into my eyes and said, "At all costs."

"But that explosion in the caboose!" said the dandy, half rising.

Fancy Collar laid a hard hand on the thin city man's shoulder. "That was no explosion, sir. It was from the engine, I assure you. The storm is playing tricks on all our senses."

Other voices chimed in, but I stood, hoping to strike fast. "Don't listen to these men," I said. "They're not railroad employees, they're thieves who blew the safe in the caboose!"

I reached to knock Fancy Collar's gun free, but he was ready for me and spun with my effort, slamming my right temple with the butt of his revolver. It was a hard knock, enough to daze me. I sensed he'd taken my gun, then patted me quickly but didn't find my sheath knife. At least I didn't think so—hard to know when your head's ringing like a church bell.

"Now folks, I know this might seem harsh," he said. "But this fellow's been trouble since we began our journey. We'd been warned about him . . ."

"No," I said, but it came out garbled, as if I had a mouthful of wet cornmeal.

Fancy Collar kept talking. "Folks, I need you to trust me. We all must remain calm. I ask you to stay in your seats while my men and I tend to the engine crew and assess the damage. Might be we'll be on our way soon, you never can tell. But for now, the safest place for all is right here. As for him," Fancy Collar looked at me and half-grinned. "We'll lock him where he can't hurt anyone—in the caboose."

"No!" I shouted again, this time managing something closer

to what the word should sound like. It didn't have any effect, save for attracting another quick clubbing. Back to the dizzying darkness I've grown familiar with. The last feeling I recall, I was being dragged.

CHAPTER FIVE

The rank tang of woodsmoke filled my nose, and teased me out of my clubbed stupor, coughing and retching. The smoke might have wakened me, but when I opened my eyes I saw no fire, only near darkness. Muffled screams and frantic, barking shouts yanked me to my feet. The cold, gray light allowed me to see the dull outline of shapes. Tendrils of smoke curled in the air, thickening with each second.

I pawed out with my hands for something to grab onto. The smoke grew denser. I was desperate to breathe, but felt as if my windpipe was being cinched by a noose of fire. Where was the smoke coming from? Did the little woodstove overturn? Did the pipe get too hot and ignite the tarred roof? I shook my head as if a bee were irking me. All that did was make the chimes in my head clang again like church bells.

I coughed and heard shouts from somewhere off to my right. I staggered in that direction, scraps of earlier commotion coming back to me. Then I recalled what had happened. I'd been having it out with that damned man when something had conked my bean. Something was said about the caboose . . . locking me in the caboose? Is that where I was?

The shouts grew louder. I heard pounding and rattling. My palms slapped the door, telling me I'd made it to the end of the car, though which end I wasn't certain, and I also felt the heat. Not so severe I couldn't keep my hand on the door as I groped for the handle, but there was definitely fire beyond.

I heaved myself out the door and was greeted with a gust of smoke in my face, then saw flames and a black cloud boiling up out of the train car door before me. Yes, I had been dragged to the caboose.

And the car before me was the passenger car . . . and it was on fire! I heard the screams of those inside, and that did more than a face full of cold water to snap me out of my foolish stupor.

I fumbled with the hot-to-the-touch steel handle of the door, grinding my teeth to powder, which did nothing for my stinging neck or my pounding head. As I pawed at the handle I looked to my left. At the ragged edge of light cast far into the snowy night, I saw a dark line, which I took to be a line of pines tailing out at the base of a slope. But it was moving, slow and sure. Elk? Horses?

Then I saw a flash of blue; it moved, then something ahead of it, a dim shape, reached out, could have sworn it was an arm, and grabbed at the blue shape.

I knew what it was—had to be. I am ashamed to admit it, but for a second I dithered. The daze I was in seems a good enough excuse, but it was the girl, her blue cape, and I hoped beyond hope that I was wrong. But my brain assumed the fleeting blue shape heading into the trees with the other darker shapes was her. I'm afraid my brain was right.

As I grappled with the scorching door handle, I squinted at the ground to the side of the train—yes, it had been trampled and pocked with indentations the size of horse hooves. Lots of them. The snow had tapered back to a spitting nuisance and I couldn't waste any more precious seconds fumbling with the car door—why didn't they unlock it from the inside?

I backed one step along the steel platform that jutted over the coupling holding the two cars. Then I did the only thing that's ever really worked for me when faced with a situation that didn't seem to have a solution—I growled like a cornered grizzly and rammed my boot heel straight at the door handle.

It wasn't my finest moment. The door shuddered, people screamed, and fists pounded the backside of the thick, wooden divider. I growled louder and gave another kick. Same thing, but the third pummeling offered sudden and satisfying results. The wood to the left of the handle split and the catch gave way. The door slammed inward, bouncing off somebody whose strangled, startled shout was cut short. I saw a spray of blood and then a whole lot of coughing, angry people pounding out of that gaping hole of smoke.

They came at me hard and fast, fire and blood in their eyes, hair smoking, sooty tears staining their cheeks, all rushing toward me.

"Get off the train!" I shouted. "Quick! We have to unhook or the caboose will go, too." They clustered before me, some of them not yet out of the burning car.

"What in the hell are you waiting for? Get out of there!" I stood to one side, leaned out over the snow, and glanced out as the firelight swallowed any sign of the riders I'd seen.

The people moved by me and climbed down into the snow, as if finally realizing the situation they were in. I guessed they considered me trouble, Fancy Collar saw to that. I would worry about that later.

"Hurry it up!" I shouted. "I need help disconnecting this car!"

I hopped down, slid in the snow, and drove my girth down on my left knee, grinding it hard against the jutting, raw end of a railroad crosstie. It felt like a knife going into my kneecap.

"What are you doing down there?"

It was the buxom woman in the bonnet, scowling at me.

"Have to unhook the caboose or the whole thing'll burn!" I shouted my response through gritted teeth.

I crawled under the cars, feeling with my bare hands at the coupling. It was a frozen mass of steel, something I'd never given much thought to before. Now that I needed to know how it worked, I was groping in the near dark with frozen fingers, feeling for something I knew nothing about.

"Anybody know how to unhook these cars?"

Nobody responded, but I got the sense they were clustered, unsure of me.

"Hey, you!"

The shout, a woman's, came to me from above. I looked up through the steel. Something dropped down close by my head, clunked, and rang as it fell into the snow beside me. "Try that— it's a steel bar, from inside the door."

It was difficult to tell who'd said it. The crackling and whooshing and smoke from above made it tricky to figure out much of anything.

"Thanks—now get out of there!"

I couldn't be certain, but I thought maybe it was the old woman with the girl who'd tossed down the bar. Didn't much care at that point. I snatched up the bar and jammed it every which way I could figure to disengage the coupling. The heat became uncomfortable, then downright brutal. I felt my wool mackinaw heat up like it was about to pop into flame.

I heard a screech and squawk, metal on metal, from above. I looked up through the smoke to see that old woman jamming her boot heel against a steel handle of some sort located down close to the floor. Of course, that was a release, had to be.

She shouted, "Try that!" then bent over into a spasm of coughing.

I managed to separate the car, more by grunts and anger and willpower—and with the help of the old lady—than by skill or wit. That steely, grinding clank as the cars separated from each other was enough to bring a thin smile to my face. But it didn't stay for long.

The car rolled away a few inches. I jammed my shoulder hard against the steel undercarriage and pushed. Never have I made such sounds. But I knew if I didn't take advantage of whatever meager amount of momentum I'd gained from unbuckling the car, the caboose would catch flame, and with it, any hopes of surviving for long out here in an early season, high-line blizzard.

To my great satisfaction, I was able to coax the caboose a couple of feet, perhaps three in all, away from the passenger car, which was moments from full fire. Maybe, I thought, the passenger car, led by the engine, could be rolled forward. But first I had to find out what was keeping the engine at a standstill.

Already, the caboose looked as if it wanted to catch fire.

I turned, looking about for the others, my freshly slammed knee wincing and offering hot, sharp pains with each move.

"Everybody okay?" I coughed the words, squinting into the night.

"What do you want?" Off to the right, it was a man's voice, maybe the dandy. The passengers stood, clustered and watching.

Before I could answer, I heard a howling voice up above, a woman's, raw with the pain only sudden fear—and too much smoke—can bring. "Where is she? Annette, where are you?"

I climbed up the steel ladder, my sore knee protesting with hot bursts. As I gained the top step, I glimpsed a figure slip straight into the burning, smoking hole that was the passenger car door. She must have leaped across the couple of feet I'd managed to pry the cars apart.

"Hey, lady!"

But it was too late, she'd already made her way into that smoky train car, fire wrapping it with angry arms. I groaned and jumped—and made it across. In I went.

My boots nudged into something on the floor at my feet, something I knew from instinct was a person. I bent low, palms out, patting, and, yes, it was indeed a person. I tried to shout but whatever air was in my mouth and pipe sucked right out when I opened my mouth. I bent low, knowing I had seconds before I flopped on top of her and died right there in that hell.

The more I fought for air, the worse it became, until I was flexing my mouth like a beached fish. I recalled advice an old Choctaw medicine man gave me once when I'd been trying to mend my saddle, destroying a harmless scrap of leather in the process. It should have been a simple repair, but for some reason that day it fought me.

The old man had been in my camp because I'd saved him from himself. That is to say he thought he needed to die by tossing himself into a half-frozen river. I didn't know this at the time, only that an old man was gasping and flopping in the water and looked like he needed help.

Anyway, he found me rassling with that scrap of hide and laid both his old horned hands on mine. He shook his head and smiled with that wrinkled apple-doll face of his. "You only fight with yourself, with something that has gone wrong. Do not take your anger out on other things." He picked up the leather. "Even this." In a couple of quick moves he made the scrap do what I'd been torturing it to do for most of an hour.

"Slow down your mind, and you will be able to breathe." His old voice echoed in my head from all those years before. When we'd finally parted ways a week or so later, I don't believe he was convinced that dying by his own hands wasn't for him. But I reasoned that a man is responsible to himself first and last. I left him to his fate, whatever he decided it was to be.

Funny how that memory slid back to me in that smoky train car. I guess I figured if I was on my way out, I'd be better off with a calm mind. I did my level best to relax, and that's when I felt the thin whistle of air leak down my throat. Sure, it was hot, smoke-filled air, but it felt pretty good. Of course, I got so excited at the thought I might not die that my throat cinched up tight again. Eventually I regained enough wind to flail around with my hands.

I managed to grab hold of her coat, two handfuls, and crab-walked backward. I bumped into something, something hot as sin, a wooden seatback, I think, then pushed away from it. I tripped, fell on my backside, then onto my back in the doorway. Enough less-heated air touched my face to revive my flagging strength. I kept on dragging the old woman.

For all that, it wasn't enough. I was about ready to expire from the heat and lack of air when hands grabbed me from behind and pulled the old woman with me, helping me, guiding me. Beside me I saw one of the passengers, the chubby merchant, though I don't know what his real occupation was. He bent down and helped me lift that woman up and across the gap between the cars.

And that's all I can recall. For a while, anyway. I lost consciousness, fell asleep, died, I don't know.

CHAPTER SIX

The next thing I recall, something was poking me in the face. A single, tiny thing, but it was insistent and steady as a well-wound pocket watch. My left eye opened first. All it saw was dark, maybe shapes. My ears worked next, heard foggy sounds, as if I'd been dunked under a freshet in a high-up mountainside. I wished that was the case.

Then the rest of me came along. My right eye opened, the sounds became distinct—voices, one of them sounded like it was laughing. And I tasted something fine and clean—fresh air.

"Hey," I tried to say. It came out sounding low and froggy. I swallowed, a hurtful task, and gave it another go. "Hello?"

Someone leaned over me. "Good morning to you." It was the fat lady. She was smiling. The thing poking me in the face was still at it.

"Manny, for heaven's sake, stop that."

The thing kept poking me. I turned my head and the thing was now poking the tip of my nose. It was the little Mexican boy.

"Manny," I said. That stopped him. Dark eyes stared at me with interest, no tears, no fear, in a soot-smudged face that looked as if it had received a half-hearted washing. He stood next to the big woman, both hands now clutching tight to her begrimed dress.

The rest of them? Were they afraid of me? I had to remind myself not to judge them. Not to judge anyone. Life should not work that way. Right then, it didn't mean I wasn't willing to judge them all to hell and back.

"He didn't mean any harm. He's curious about you, that's all."

"We all are," said another voice.

I turned my head. It was the dandy.

"And why . . ." I cleared my throat, wincing at the raw feeling. "Why are you curious about me? I am . . . was a passenger on this train like the rest of you. I don't care what you think of me."

"If you're not one of them what done this, who are you and what has happened here? You seemed to know them and . . ."

I held up a hand, and saw it was as black as if I'd been wearing fine leather gloves. "Hold on, you," I said, pushing myself to a sitting position. My head hit something halfway up, a top bunk or a shelf. I tried again, leaning out, and made it to a sitting position before I had to stop, keeping my eyes pinned on something across from me.

And that's when I saw it, the blown safe. So I was right. I must have said that out loud, because Dandy nodded, "Yes, they robbed the safe, as you said, but how did you know? That's what gives us pause."

"Mull on that pause all you like, Dandy, but I can't help you. Where's the old woman?" I asked, my eyes springing wide. I hadn't thought of her before that moment.

"If by old woman you mean me, young man, then I am right here," she said, her voice coming out in a slow croak. "Thanks to you." She leaned over from the shadows to my right. It was the old woman, the one who'd traveled with the girl in blue. She was alive, but she looked about as well as I felt. Not good in the least. Then she reached for me, grabbing my arm.

"Ma'am," I said. "I tried to tell you, I don't believe your daughter was lost in the fire."

"I've been waiting for you to wake. You said something of the sort hours ago in your sleep."

"I did? Well, I saw her. At least I think I did. She was being led away by them. On horseback. I saw blue, her cloak. I could swear it was her."

"Yes, it's true, then. I thought I saw him take her, but I hoped he was only saving her. Oh, I don't know. It's all so confusing now."

"Who?" I said. "Who took her?"

"That young man in the bowler. The boss of them."

Fancy Collar. That decided it for me.

I thought the old woman might cry then, but she didn't. She looked at me. "You did see her, though?" Her eyes searched mine, desperate for an answer.

I was not lying when I nodded. "Yes, ma'am. I'm sure of it." I knew the answer, everything she had said only confirmed the foulness of the thing I had seen. She had been taken by them. Whoever they were. She did not like them, did not know them, that much I was sure of. Had to be that way, given how put off she was by the drunken attention of Hector and the rest.

"Then why in God's name didn't you do something about it?" It was the dandy again.

I stood, my head all rubbery and bouncy inside. But I had enough momentum to lean right over him and poke a meaty finger in his birdlike chest. "I've had enough of you, you . . ."

That's when I saw Manny, the little boy, staring up at me. I wanted to drive that fist I had balled by my side right into the dandy's face, that smug, pinched know-it-all face. It was a face I'd seen in a hundred flyblown towns across the West, superior because of circumstance, if nothing else.

But the boy's eyes, staring at me, searching, maybe hoping for . . . what? Violence? No, I could not do it. I expected me and the dandy would settle his hash another time. But it didn't stop me from drilling my finger into that caved-in chest. "It was either break in that door of the train car that was on fire, the one you were in," those last three words each got a good poking, "the one you didn't help to open, I might add, or give chase to those men and the girl. And they were already heading for the treeline yonder." I gestured with my head. "On horseback, to boot." I fancy the dandy didn't look so sure of himself, his nose not so upturned and sniffy as it was.

"Horseback?" said the chubby merchant man.

I nodded. "Yep. And that means that they had someone waiting, someone who blocked the track with whatever the engine hit." That's when it came to me. I stood straighter, looking at them all. "Anyone check on the engineers?"

They looked down. The buxom woman sniffled. "Dead, they'd been . . ." She sobbed and didn't finish.

The chubby man said, "They've been stabbed. Their throats . . ." He, too, saw the boy, and left off from telling the rest.

I understood. They'd used no bullets, no sound to alert the passengers.

"And the tracks?"

"A couple of sizable trees. Dragged a distance, I'd say."

"Did you shift them?" I said.

The man shook his head. "Not possible."

"But the fire . . ."

He nodded, and oddly enough, smiled a tired smile. They were all tired. It felt as if the entire world was tired. I knew I was exhausted.

"Why is that funny?" I asked.

"We were all out there." He glanced at the dandy. "Well, most of us. Throwing snow on the fire. Then the wind slowed and heavy snow fell again. Before we knew it the flames on the passenger car sputtered, went out. We've been taking shifts, keeping an eye on it in case it decides to come back to life."

CHAPTER SEVEN

As daylight crept in through the caboose's few sooty windows, I saw the effects of the previous night on the faces of my fellow passengers. No one escaped having their hair singed. Clothing bore burn marks, the chubby merchant wore a bloody rag tied around his head, and the burly woman and the dandy both held wads of dripping snow to welts and blisters on their arms and hands.

Excluding my presence, the caboose wasn't large enough for four adults and one child to stretch out and sleep. I expect they'd have to take turns on the shelves intended for freight.

The blast the bad men had used to gain entry to the safe had been contained and did little more than fling open the heavy steel door. What was so important they felt it necessary to murder the engineers and try to kill the passengers—and abscond with a young woman—innocents all?

"How long was I . . . asleep?" I looked at the chubby man and no one else.

He shrugged. "A few hours, I don't really know. It could have been a year, for all I know. We're all exhausted." He looked particularly rough, squinting as if the scant light caused him pain.

"Annette . . ." muttered the old woman as she stared out a grimy window. I tried to think of a solution, tried to slow the spinning in my head. It helped to concentrate on one thing, a face, a hook on the wall, the little woodstove that felt to be doing its job well enough.

I cleared my throat. I knew what had to be done. "I don't need to tell you all that the snow and cold temperatures won't be good things. More than likely we'll be out here a few days, at least until folks at the other end, in Deerhoof, figure out the train's late. Then they'll send someone to see what the holdup is."

The fat woman nodded. "How long do you really think it might be?"

I rubbed my face, careful to not drag soot into my already stinging eyes. "Well, we weren't but a few hours late when all this happened. And they aren't expecting us for another day or so, by my reckoning. So it could be . . . two days?"

"More like never!" growled the dandy. He caught my eye and looked down at his shoes.

"That's not helpful, fella."

"What do you suggest we do, then?"

"I'm guessing the tender car behind the engine still has a goodly supply of wood. Should feed this stove all right."

The chubby man nodded. "I thought of that, but it's cut long, no way we can fit it in this little stove. There's some chunk coal here, but that won't last long."

"Might be for warmth you'll have to build a bonfire outside. Keep it fed, not a bad idea anyway. The smoke will let the railroad folks know where you're at."

"You keep saying 'you' as if you won't be here."

"I won't," I said. Everyone turned to stare at me, even the little boy. The old woman broke off from mumbling the girl's name and looked at me.

"Where do you think you're going?" It was the dandy again. Soon enough, I figured, I'd dispense with the kindness I'd shown him in not driving one of my ham hands into his gawky face, little boy watching or no.

"I have to track those bast—, ah," I caught sight of the boy's eyes again. "Those bad men."

"But you said yourself they're on horseback."

"Yeah, I expect, like the rest of us, they hoped luck would keep the snow away for a few days more. Those horses are going to be more trouble than they're worth in this weather." I looked out the window, smearing a spot to peer through. "We got a pile of it and it's still coming down, hammer and tong."

"What are your plans, then?" said the chubby man.

"Track them on foot. Their trail should be visible even with the fresh snow on top. It will be a wide, ragged line of hoofprints. I don't guess they'd be doubled up, at least not in the snow, too hard on the animals. There were three men we know of. At least another one who brought the horses and dragged those trees across the track. And then perhaps another horse for . . . the girl."

I didn't have the heart to smile at the woman, but I tried to look as though I was filled with hope. Nothing could be more wrong, though. I didn't give the girl much of a chance. The dismal looks on the faces of the other passengers showed they felt the same way.

Judging from how they treated the engineers and passengers, those filthy men would kill her when they tired of her company. Kill her and leave her body up there somewhere on the pass to freeze, to be picked over by wolves or coyotes, wolverines, lord knows what else. The thought made me wince inside.

"You're in no shape to set off on foot in this, especially not into the mountains. You'll freeze to death." It was the chesty woman.

The dandy made a quick grunting sound as if he'd like nothing better than for me to expire in the snow. I ignored him. And then he spoke again. "What do we do? We'll starve!"

"You use your brains, Dandy. Any of you hunt?" I looked

around but there were no nodding heads. What a day, I thought. And it had barely begun.

"Look," I said. "I don't have time to hunt for you, but scout for guns, see if anything got overlooked. In the meantime, take stock of whatever food there is on board. When it's safe, rummage in the ashes of the passenger car and the engine, see if you can turn up anything. Work together, only eat what's necessary to get through. Trust me, you need water far more than you need food. And since there's plenty of snow to melt, you'll be fine. Stay warm, drink water, work together, and you'll be fine. I have to go, but I'll be back as soon as I can."

"What if you don't come back?" The fat woman said it.

I tried to sound reassuring and lowered my voice. "Well, ma'am, I don't want to think about that any more than you do." I glanced at the window. "The sky doesn't look any too welcoming. I'd say we're going to get more snow anytime now. This is a lull. But the storm can't last forever. If you really can't take it or . . ."

The chubby man finished for me. "If they don't come for us in a timely manner," he said.

I nodded, "Yeah, then bundle up and follow the tracks eastward."

The dandy and the fat woman both looked at me as if they were dumb cows. I sighed. "That way," I said pointing east. "The direction we were headed. That's likely where help from the railroad will come from anyway."

I had a thought then, and pushed my way past them. "Might want to start on getting what small wood you can for the stove before the storm kicks up again." They nodded and made their way out the end of the caboose and helped each other down the steel rungs to the ground.

The old woman stayed behind, still looking out the window. I didn't know what to say to her, and doubted she'd believe me if

I promised to find the girl.

I eased past her and rummaged in a pile of goods and gear they'd tossed in the back corner, too close to the potbelly stove for my liking, and then I found it.

My carpetbag full of books. One end had been torn, likely in the blast, nearly pulled apart at a seam, but it held. Damn good bag.

I opened the toggle buttons and spread the mouth wide.

"What are you hiding?"

The voice came from behind me. I turned. It was the old woman.

"Not hiding anything, ma'am. These are mine."

She looked closer. "Books?" She gave me a long inspection, as if she was trying to figure out what sort of critter I was. Then she surprised me. Her eyes focused, seemed sharper. "I won't let them burn, young man. We're not savages, after all. And besides," she reached into the bag and hefted one, an abused copy of a translation of *The Divine Comedy* by Dante Alighieri. "How appropriate," she said. "I may need something to pass the time so I won't have to hear that insufferable whelp whine any more. The one you call 'Dandy.' " She smiled, but I knew it was painful for her to muster.

"I'll do my best to find her, ma'am."

She nodded. "I believe you will, young man." She looked back at the bag of books. "Annette is all I have." Her lip trembled and her red-rimmed eyes teared, spilling over. "She's my niece. Her father died recently . . . a terrible accident. In Seattle. She's an orphan now. We're all each other has, you see."

"I understand, ma'am." I didn't know what else to say.

She made it easy for me and laid the book back in the bag. "I was a private tutor for families of standing for many years back East. I know the value of a good book. From the looks, you have a stack of fine ones here."

"Much obliged, ma'am. I . . . I should get going. I found what I needed." I pulled out a small cloth sack, untied it, and slid out a thick wad of peppered buffalo jerky. I grabbed a quarter of it, stuffed it into my coat pocket, then handed her the rest. "Share this with the others as you see fit, ma'am."

"Oh no, no, you should have it all with you. It's yours, you'll need it."

"I have plenty, ma'am." I patted my pocket, pulling nearly the last thing from the bag that wasn't books—the knitted thick-wool red socks. I'd bought them for Jack, but my gloves were likely gone, lost in the passenger car, I guessed.

I'd use these for my hands or feet or both, alternately as time and the elements demanded. I still had my hat, though the brim was charred at the edges like paper pulled from a campfire, but it would serve me well enough, I reckoned.

The hat, the socks, my hip knife, and my possibles bag, a buckskin pouch I wore around my neck, were all I had. The possibles bag would be the most valuable thing to me, another thing Jack taught me to carry. It contained various bits and bobs useful at one time or another on the trail: a few store-bought fishhooks, a coil of tough twine, a flint and steel, and enough tinder for a half-dozen campfires, if I was cautious. Most important of all, a handful of prime coffee beans.

I do love my coffee and while these weren't enough to grind up for liquid coffee, I have found that chewing on a bean now and again is a helpful way to get a milder version of the sensation I so like about coffee—a complex blend of taste and smell and overall good feeling. That's my weakness, among others, I'm sure.

I also carry three spare shells for the Schofield—which the bastards took from me. It was a decent weapon and I hoped they wouldn't lob it into the snow somewhere along the trail. It had served me well for a number of years and I had no intention of parting with it.

Then I remembered the Colt I'd taken from Hector—where was that? I'd tucked it half-under a cushion in my seat, intending to give it back once we'd reached Deerhoof. I doubted it was still useful or even still there, but I'd check before I left the train. Then another gun popped to mind.

"Ma'am? You recall that derringer the drunk fella had?"

She nodded, then shook her head. "I'm sorry, but that man, the one who . . . who took her," her lip trembled, but she soldiered on. "He took it back from us when you were talking with the engineer."

I sighed and nodded. Not like such a tiny gun would be of much use anyway. But any gun is better than none when you're facing a knot of snakes.

"What's your name, young man?"

"Folks call me Roamer, ma'am."

"Well, Godspeed to you, Roamer. Sounds not unlike Homer, my favorite author." I could see she was fighting the urge to cry again. She didn't have to tell me more about the girl to know what she meant to her. Neither of us had to talk about what we both hoped was not happening to the girl somewhere out there in the mountains.

I nodded once, touched my hat brim, and climbed out of the caboose. Unlike Homer, I wasn't in the mood for sharing stories, though at that moment I would have gladly traded places with a traveling bard for anything other than what I was facing.

My brief inspection of the charred, smoking innards of the passenger car failed to turn up the confiscated Colt, or anything else. My small war bag had burned down into something unrecognizable, and with it any hopes I had of finding more warm clothing. I climbed down and surveyed the north side of the track. A long line of indentations curved away in the new snowfall upward toward the mountains.

The snap of the windblast raked my face like the frozen claws of some great ice beast. I set out.

CHAPTER EIGHT

As I expected, the reprieve in the weather had been but a lull. I looked back once, before I lost sight of the snow-mired, still-smoking train. Shapes of the few passengers moved about the wreck in the gray morning as snow drifted down. I tried not to look, didn't want the dandy to have the satisfaction of thinking I was afraid. Truth was, I would have gladly trudged the mile back to the train from the treeline to punch him on the nose. Petty of me, I know. But a fella like that chafes a fella like me.

The snow out on the sweep of land leading from the train to the trees was deceptive in its depth. I expected to sink in, and I did, not only because I'm not a tiny man, but also because the storm's attendant winds had carved drifts at times taller than me.

It took too long to get to the treeline. I paused to catch my breath and give that pained knee a rest. At that moment, I had no idea how I'd catch up with those killers and thieves. I took small comfort in the notion that their horses would not be ambitious enough to climb uphill for hours in snow grazing their chests.

While my breathing evened, I took stock of my situation. The cold air and pelting snow did its best to keep me from wallowing in the thudding of my head's pain. I was ill-equipped for this venture, likely as ill-equipped as the thieves were well-equipped.

In my state it was easy to see only the raw and rough of a

situation. But I had plenty of reason to be hopeful, too. I was alive, reason enough for optimism. My vision was clearing—the two of everything I'd been seeing were melting into one fuzzy sight—useful considering I was trying to follow a cold trail covered with a dumping of new snow.

"Has to be a smarter way to live than this, Roamer," I mumbled to myself. It didn't do any good. I've said it a number of times over the years and yet there I was, stumbling through knee-deep snow, driving my way through chest-high drifts, following the faint line of depressions made by the horses' hooves at dusk the night before.

The trees, a forest of spruce, thickened as the gentle flanks of the Bitterroots rose before me. Those trees would provide respite from the wind, for a time, anyway. The breeze quickened and became emboldened the farther I walked from the train. I looked back once more before entering a narrow cleft in the trees, but a rise in the middle of the plain I'd crossed blocked the smoking wreck from me. I thought of a hundred and more things I should have done for the small group of passengers.

Their lack of abilities left me bothered. What was wrong with the world, I wondered, when grown men looked to others to take care of them? Asking for help is fine, but that dandy was a grown man as fearful and defensive as a drunk who realizes he's met his match in an alley.

Sadly, he's the sort of fellow I've come across many times before. He'd be quick to blame others, and would do his best to claw up what he would feel was his "fair share" of any rations they could stockpile. He is the reason democracies cave in on themselves.

I smacked my hands together to flow the blood in my fingers. Seeing the red woolen socks made me think of Maple Jack. And thinking of Jack resulted in me smiling, despite the fact that I missed my gloves. All my clothes, in fact. They had burned in

the passenger car. I thought the bag would make a decent pil-
low on the journey, and now they were burned. At least I had
Jack's socks for mittens. Could be worse.

I set my course, squinting through the snow and into the
trees where the outline of the trail could still be seen. I
continued that practice, setting landmarks aligning with the
trail. Should the trail become lost to me in the snow, I might
still get a sense of the party's general direction. As I slow-
stepped through the snow, I set to work on puzzling out the
logistics of this tangle.

We'd been gone nearly two days, and that means we'd be
expected in Deerhoof tomorrow. The railroad authorities would
no doubt be aware of the storm and when their train failed to
arrive at the expected hour, let alone on the expected day, they
would be concerned enough to send out a party of rescuers.
That was my hope, anyway.

Another smile came unbidden to my face as I heard Jack's
voice in my head: "Hope in one hand, mess in the other, see
which fills faster."

I'd always found hope to be useless unless accompanied by
effort. And Jack would put effort into finding me, I know. He
would be waiting at the Deerhoof depot, Ol' Mossback, his
trusty mule, standing still, his dozy look and drooped ears not
revealing the fact that he was a steadfast and true beast with
trigger-quick speed when startled.

Mossy would be laden with Jack's winter goods, two big panniers of Jack's own devising that allowed him to also ride atop
the stalwart beast when the mood grabbed him. Jack would be
leading Tiny Boy, my Percheron, another steadfast beast with
more grit than any horse I've ever met.

When I wasn't where I was supposed to be when I was supposed to be there, and given the blizzard, Jack would grow
cantankerous and concerned, in that order. Then he would

listen to the railroad folks, tell them train travel was a dicey way to get about any time of year, and especially foolish when snow was a possibility.

They would stare at him as if he were a crazy man down from the mountains (who could blame them?). He would then declare them all fools incapable of finding their hats with both hands. Then he would study the map in his head—the man knows the Northern Rockies better than most folks know their children. Then he'd peel away from the group and set a course that would rendezvous with me.

How that was going to happen when Jack had no idea of my location was beyond my mental capacities at the moment. With each step I took, the inside of my head thudded like cannon fire. Despite my previous thoughts on hope, I indulged in some, thinking how nice it would be if Jack were to find me before I was a frozen dead man.

For the remainder of the daylight hours, I walked. Each step, I chose to believe brought me closer to the girl, Annette, and her captors. While I grunted along I chewed on the various no-tions jumping and bubbling in my head. The girl, her pretty face, her eyes. Then her old aunt, a tough woman with a core of iron. Then the dandy, a worm of a man. What had made him that way? Surely he didn't want to be so smarmy. Maybe I had no right to judge him.

Then the others, the jowly man, the big-chested woman, and her charge, the little Mexican boy, Manny. Now there was one to ponder. Quiet as a mouse, no emotion showing on that face, dark eyes wide and studying. I wagered there was a whole lot more going on behind those eyes than anyone credited him for.

And finally, I settled on a topic I could no longer ignore: I gave thought to Fancy Collar and Hector and the bald, ginger-whiskered man.

Who were they? Why hadn't I been more cautious? Why

hadn't I trusted my gut about them? It had rarely led me astray—except when I overate at the stewpot. Thinking back on them and the brief, eventful journey, I realized they had no more looked or acted like railroad men than I did. I was a fool, I determined, and had to carry some of the blame for this mess.

My only hope lay in following their trail, a trail I saw with a stiffening of my back, was quickly disappearing from sight. The faint depressions were vanishing not only under the snow and wind, but under the dark day's surrender to dusk. I needed to find a spot to make camp. All the while, the snow rose higher and higher.

I found a sizable pine. From past experience I knew there would be a natural cavity around the base of the trunk somewhat free of snow where I could den for the night. I had my big coat, the sheepskin collar pulled high and tight about my neck. It did a serviceable job covering my ears, but only if I didn't move my head much. Fortunately, I hadn't needed to for most of the afternoon.

Getting down under the tree's lowest, broad branches was the trick. I nudged down with my right boot, holding the swaying branches at head height for support. In this manner, by sweeping my leg back and forth, I was able to carve a rounded path. Figured I'd do as much as I could standing up, then duck down and burrow in there on my hands and knees.

I would get colder and wetter doing so, but that couldn't be helped. Before I crawled in, I ranged about the tight-packed clot of trees and snapped off as many branches as I was able to find. I planned on coaxing a fire large enough to warm my hands and feet, maybe a little water.

The stick gathering took longer than I would have liked, and I was tuckered out clear through to my bones and shivering. I could not stop my teeth from clacking. I was also losing daylight.

Full dark comes quick in October in the mountains on a gray day.

I didn't want to fritter what little advantage nature had offered, so I shoved the branches ahead of me and squirmed and crawled my way down the meager tunnel, my knee the only hot thing on me, pulsing out pain like hammer blows on a thumb. I made it to the center of the tree, and clunked my head on the trunk, truth be told. Then I hunched up, blowing on my hands. I fancy I looked like a squirrel working on an acorn.

I realized no amount of huffing on my fingertips would warm them. The light down in the breezy little snow cave was pinching off fast. I needed to kindle that fire. I heard the wind sighing, my own breaths stuttering in and out, clouding then vanishing as I worked.

Dragging out my possibles bag until it hung outside my layers of wool and buckskin took more time than it ought. My wood-stiff fingers managed to pinch out my flint and steel without spilling the rest of the bag. Tinder was another matter. I held the mouth of the buckskin sack up to my own mouth and felt with my tongue the soft wad of birch curls and wool I kept in there. I pulled it out with my teeth. My hands shook so I had to use my teeth again to tease apart a smidgen of the fuzzy, dry tinder.

Next I gathered twigs and needles from close to the hard slope of the trunk. I leaned against that, found I couldn't do what I needed to—kindle a fire—while leaning, and bent forward. Good thing, too, or I might have dozed off right there and not revived again until St. Peter clunked me on the bean with his harp.

I arranged the fluff of tinder, though my hands shook with such violence it took a month. Next I crunched up dry material I'd gathered from the tree base, layered larger sticks atop that, and left an opening at the base where I cuffed my steel against the flint.

Finally, after what felt like weeks, a spark grabbed hold of a thin hair of wool and traveled along it like a walking glow bug. I bent low and blew. Not low enough. The spark winked out. Some sort of grunty animal squeal boiled right up out of my throat.

I don't know as I've ever heard myself make such a sound before, but then again never have I been that damned cold and incapable of sparking fire. Would that I had store-bought lucifers. I curse myself for not being a smoker—a first for me, I tell you.

With a stiff hand I cuffed the delicate structure of sticks and dry needles aside and before I lost all feeling, once more I fumbled the flint and steel into my fingers and slammed them together over and over above the little wad of tinder. It worked. Sparks snagged, racing in their peculiar way around the tendrils of debris. Before I knew it my thick fingers had nudged twigs and needles and other dry junk gently over the catching glow. Smoke became sparks became darting cat tongues of flame became bold, though still small, whips of fire, devouring the tinder like a tiny, starved beast.

I had intended to keep the fire small, demure enough to warm my hands and a pinch of water. But already it had climbed up face-height and threatened to back me up with its vigor.

"Careful what you wish for," I reminded myself. My grim chuckle turned into a small cough. I kept the fire down to a manageable height, feeding it with snapped sticks from the snag of branches I'd gathered. It liked them and wanted more. But control, even though I was cold and shivery and miserable, was something I could not afford to be without, else the tree might catch fire and me with it. And what good would that do?

As my face warmed and my fingers pulsed with the pain only

brutal cold leaves behind, I thought of hot water, perhaps a little pine needle tea? I liked the thought. Trouble is, I didn't have anything to heat the water in. My thoughts roved from my hat to my hands, neither of which could sustain a cupful of fire-hot water.

But hot water was one thing I could survive the lack of more than most. I had plenty of snow. Still, it would have been nice to have a tin cup. I've had luck making suitable vessels from bark, moss, burls from trees, hollowed apples—none of which I had at the moment. I thought again of using my hat, but it was a bad idea and I didn't want to risk scorching it further.

I'd scare up something more functional on the trail tomorrow. For tonight, I reasoned, I'd eat snow, nibble a bite of jerky, and do my best to not set the tree alight. Little danger of that as my fire was once more a meager creature and my wood supply scant.

Wind, low and slicing, weaseled its way into my half-hearted snow cave. I call it half-hearted because a true snow cave is a warm affair, but only if the builder has the luxury of time and coherence. I was knackered and soon found myself nodding, my mittened hands outstretched over the flames, wagging down toward it. I felt the heat once and yanked my hand back in time to prevent scorching a hole right though one of those red socks. So much for Jack's gift. I'd make it up to him somewhere down the trail.

I finally realized I was losing the battle, so I left the paltry flames to pinch out on their own, leaned back against the trunk, and hunkered deep in my coat. My collar was tugged up tight about my ears and face, my hat down low, and my arms wrapped as if I were trying to hug myself to sleep. I tried to pull my legs up close to my chest but that knee was still sore from driving it against the rail tie. I bent it as much as I could, and that's about all I remember. That and the crosswinds slicing through the tree branches above my head.

Snow must have drifted higher about the base of the tree because while I heard the wind above, I felt less of it reaching me from gaps around the base. I've spent many miserable nights in unforgiving weather in the past, but this was one of the worst. My last thought before sleep made off with my mind was how I hoped I wouldn't wake up dead. Because that, to quote Jack, would make me mighty mad.

CHAPTER NINE

Warmth such as I hadn't felt in ages spread over my face. I smiled, and stayed like that long enough to tick through everything that had happened over the past couple of days. That wiped away my smile. I sighed, forced open an eye, and heard a cracking sound. A flash of fear shivered through me—I had visions of branches crashing down, unbelievable gobs of snow dropping, pounding me to pulp.

And then I learned what the cracking sound was—ice had crusted from my stiff, raised sheepskin collar to my face. I jerked and the thin shell crumbled. I breathed deep, scrunched my face, and wondered about opening my second eye. I decided it would be the prudent thing to do. Time to drag myself into this new day.

The sunlight needled in through the tree's upper branches and began to warm me. I'd no idea when I balled up beneath this mighty pine that I'd been facing east enough to gain benefit from the early sun's warming might. A little something to be thankful for. Maybe that's all we all need at the outset of each day—a little something. I'd cogitate on that later. Right then, I had to figure out how to unbend my limbs.

I was certain, cold as I was, that if I bent any part of me, arms, legs, ears, nose, neck, I'd find myself with a dismal stack of snapped body parts and no way to reattach them. Fanciful thoughts have plagued my early mornings for as long as I can recall. That's how I know I'm not yet awake.

I gave it another minute or so, breathing in deep of the morning mountain air, taking it in low in my lungs, pushing it up and out again. That revived me and I shook myself much as a dog after dunking in a river. Well, perhaps with not as much gusto. It worked, and within seconds my head and arms were freed from their icy armor. It cracked apart and tinkled to the snow about me like shards of the thinnest glass. If it were not so cold, I might have admired the prettiness of it longer. But my teeth commenced their clattering and my hand began such a palsied dance I wondered if I'd been savaged by a hydrophobic wolf in the night.

When I emerged from my raw burrow, I gasped at the sight: The sky was bluer than even that pretty girl's cloak, nearly as pretty as her eyes. I swayed on my knees for a long moment, no matter the throbbing, taking in the splendor of mountains decked in winter finery.

"Nothing can possibly ever again be this pretty," I whispered, knowing I am prone of a morning to sudden emotion. And then my pretty morning moment melted. I was once more a big, ailing man ill-equipped for my situation and half-frozen, hip-deep in snow on a quest for a fair maiden. Epic poems have been written on wobblier premises.

Rise, oh unworthy man, and set forth once more. For that is all you can do in life. I told myself this and too many other weak, dandified notions. In such a manner I was able to perk myself enough to stand, take stock of my person, and scoop a mitten full of snow. In short order I set forth once more, swinging slow and steady along the still barely visible trail left by my quarry.

Ah, the things a body will do to survive into another day, I told myself. But before the next day dawned, I would have cause to reconsider such daft, albeit thin, dreams.

CHAPTER TEN

I am not one to laze about of a morning. I'd rather rise and, if not shine, at least glow. Coffee helps put a shine on most of my mornings. Since I did not have the ability to conjure hot coffee, I pinched up two of my precious coffee beans and crunched them to paste, one bean at a time. The taste requires dogged dedication. I savored the bitter bite the beans offered, and with reluctance filled my mouth with snow, followed with more snow. For dessert, a handful of snow.

Despite my fondness for coffee, it never fails to amaze me what reviving effects water has on a body. It wasn't long before I felt good enough to hum softly to myself as I stepped slow and long through the snow.

The day was turning off warm. If it continued, I'd have to keep an eye open for snow slumping from on high. Enough had fallen in the blizzard that it was a possibility. The sun baked itself into my good graces, as did the wind, by lessening its presence. It wasn't long before I unbuttoned my coat. It wouldn't do to get sweated up, only to freeze again in a few hours when the winter sun pinched out.

I spent the day doing the same thing over and over, eyeballing the terrain ahead, which grew steeper by the hour, setting my course based on what I hoped was still the trail of the murdering kidnappers and their captive. They had been on horseback and their trail bore that out.

Instead of switchbacking toward the pass I suspected they

were headed for, as someone on foot might do, they had traveled across the grain, so to speak, angling from east to west in a long cut. This would get them to the pass with less risk of toppling a horse down the mountainside from too steep an angle.

By midafternoon my breathing was something I had to work at. Thinner air up high made each step more of a labor than the one before. Well, that and my stubbornness at not surrendering to stop for a rest. Every time I wanted to, that girl's kind face flickered into my mind. As quickly, the dread on her aunt's face nibbled at me. I scooped more snow and kept trudging in my rough path along the mountain's side.

At timberline, the trees thinned, grew more stunted, and I wondered what I was going to huddle beneath that night. I was still low enough on the slopes to spy outcrops and jags of boulders that looked promising as shelter. I guessed I had less than an hour before it would be too difficult to see. I didn't want to make camp in the dark once more.

Instead of continuing my upward trek, I angled slightly westward and downslope toward what appeared to be one of the last copses of trees I'd see for a while. None of them were taller than me, but they were clumped to one side of a cluster of boulders. The largest rock, smaller than a tarped freight wagon, jutted over two others, the cluster appearing placed in such a manner by intention.

The closer I drew to it, the more pleased I became. I determined it would serve my needs nicely for the night. I was wiped, as Jack likes to say after he's put in a few hours at the chopping block. It was only when I edged my way between smaller, attendant boulders at its base did I begin to wonder if I might not be the only critter who saw promise in the jumble of stone.

There was no fresh sign, no tracks or scat, to prove my hunch correct, but that tickle feeling down low at the base of my neck had proven itself useful more times than I can recall, so I paid attention to it. I approached the gape of rock, my head canted forward, hat pushed back. I wanted to hear above the slight whistle of wind leaking downslope and through the rocks. I paused, but heard nothing.

The hole was not quite a cave, not quite exposed. But it was promising and would save me time in carving out digs for myself. I leaned back against a boulder, the face of it still warm from sunlight, and surveyed the little grotto. I would not be able to stand up inside, but then again I had no intention of standing all night. I was ready for sleep. But not yet.

I kept myself awake yawning and stretching, eager to make camp. If anything else came along looking for a cozy spot, I'd gladly share as long as it didn't sink fang into me. I was too tired to give it more thought beyond that.

I moved as though I had lead boots, but with more reason to feel cheerful than the previous evening. I still had daylight, less snow coming down in gusts every which way, and a clot of stunty trees stood close at hand, several of them wind-stripped and dead. Perfect for keeping me warm without me having to kill any of them. Cold as I was, I reckoned anything that could survive so high up in such an unforgiving spot deserved to be left alone to carry on. At least while it was alive. A dead tree? That's fair game.

I slid my big Green River skinner from its sheath and commenced to lopping branches. Before long I had an admirable stack beside me in the snow. I considered carrying them, but found it easier to toss them the ten feet or so into the hollow where I intended to build the fire. It was a good spot, well-protected from pestering wind. Perhaps I'd live through this mess after all. I smirked at the thought, given how many times over the years I'd found myself in similar hard spots. And yet, here I be.

One branch, midway up the trunk, bulged out, bellying into a swell nearly as big as my two cupped palms. I'd seen such burls through the years but usually on sizable trees in forests. That this tree had developed one was of interest to me. Though I am no naturalist, I am naturally curious. I tapped it with my knife, raising an eyebrow at the subsequent hollow thunk I heard. This could be a most welcome discovery, indeed.

I hatcheted with the knife a hand's width above and the same below the burl. This provided me enough of a handle on either side of the knob to grasp the affair firmly in two hands.

If all went well, I thought, grinning like a child at Christmastime, I may have a vessel. And a vessel, even one of wood, broadened my meager possibilities tenfold.

I finished savaging the dead trees among the living and, satisfied I had enough wood to keep me comfortable for a few hours, I tossed the remaining sticks to the spot I'd build the fire, taking care not to toss the hunk of wood with the burl.

I rolled head-size rocks over and nudged them into place with my boot. Once the fire spot had been built, and with the fire kindled, I set to work inspecting the boll. I still had a good half hour of daylight, enough to let me poke the knife's tip into the heart of the knot, to see if I could exploit the shape to suit my needs.

I was pleased to find that the center, once I probed past a bark-and-wood-grain skin less than a half-inch thick, was mostly hollow. I widened the top, rounding the opening enough to probe the cavity with a finger. I roughed it open wider, perhaps the diameter of a dollar coin, and was able to keep doing such. Within ten minutes I had breached the skin sufficiently that I could stuff three of my fat fingers in there. And that's saying something.

Next I dug, scraped, and scooped at the inside of the boll as best as I could, making the interior as smooth as time allowed.

Soon enough the test came. I set two more sticks of wood on the fire and stuffed the burl with snow. I rubbed the outside of the bowl with melting snow. This would help prevent the burl from burning through, if not scorching. I would have to keep it wet as possible inside and out, though.

It proved large enough to hold maybe three mouthfuls of water, or rather snow that I would melt into water. I held the full burl over flame, not daring to lower it too close, lest I end up cupless once more. The wood caught fire twice, mostly tendrils of bark still attached, but soon the snow melted, and sent up the faintest traces of steam. The water was heating and I pictured a steaming bowl of soup, chunked with chicken or beef, topped with sprinkled spices, and perhaps a few moist dumplings.

A smoky, burning smell pulled me from my reverie. The bowl had caught flame again. I jerked the burl away from the fire quickly. It was fine, barely scorched, and wet through, which was my intent. That would help protect it as I heated water. Nature had left the tiny gift for me, and I would have to be careful as well as grateful.

A raven sawtoothed his way across the late-day sky, which shed the last of its gray storm cloak even as the sun vanished. Despite the rough accommodations, I felt more at ease on this night than I had since my last night with the freighting outfit, alone, encamped by a slow stream, the oxen grazing in the near silence.

Given my efforts of the day, it was odd that I found myself unable to doze when I most wanted to. The relative comfort of the fire, the extra bite of jerky I'd allowed myself, the warmed snowmelt in my burl-carved cup should all have conspired to promote a deep slumber. Instead, a riot of thoughts bedeviled me.

Notions warred in my mind of the girl, the train, the

scoundrels, the fire, my books, the old woman, the damnable dandy, and, tromping hell-for-leather over it all, my friend Maple Jack atop Ol' Mossback and with Tiny Boy keeping pace. You'd think such a jumble would render me low, even if in a fitful sleep. But it didn't. I kept thinking and thinking.

Was I still on their trail or had I lost it? I'd marked the pass above and westerly of me as the surest gap they'd make for. It lorded above this rift I'd been hiking through, its passage lower than the others to the southwest and northeast along this spine of the Bitterroots. At least I think that's where I was.

I've never worried about exactly where I was, according to man-drawn maps, anyway. I prefer to rove the land up and down, around and beside waters that run and waters that sit right where they've always been. I've rambled along masses of ice in the highest mountain passes that stay put, even in winter. I've camped along the surf line of oceans, soothed by the never-ending roll and splash of waves.

I've seen a good bit of such things and I never tire of them. I do tire of clusters of houses, buildings cobbled together by people who traveled fair distances to dig and gouge and burn and blast and carve up the land I love.

Then they define it with lines only mapmakers and bankers and surveyors get excited about. But those lines are powerful. They keep out folks and critters who once passed freely through these places. And they keep in the suspicious, bitter men and women who assigned them, huddling together in towns. And they call themselves content. Perhaps they are—who am I to judge them?

But being around greedy people has an unfortunate effect on me, so much so that I find myself fed up, and then I have to get away from them and find the peace of solitude once more. I speak, of course, of the folks who deserve such raw treatment. Not the few I've come to admire. Hard of me, to be sure, but my opinion is mine, and other folks can have theirs.

These prickly thoughts finally drove me to sleep, a rag of a man wrung out and tossed damp to the rocky ground. I reckon I was so exhausted I could have slept through about anything. And that's what I did—and it nearly did me in.

CHAPTER ELEVEN

The sound woke me before the feeling did. Ten freight trains passing by from all directions. And as loud as that rushing, pummeling was, a bigger din wrapped itself around the train sounds, a sort of whooshing, sliding, scraping that can only be made by nature itself. And then came the pounding.

I felt as though I were laid out on a bed the size of a mountain meadow and giant hands from above jostled and jounced the blankets on which I lay. They jerked me upward such that I had no ability to move on my own. I could only endure the thrashing.

Then the trains thundered by, their deafening, deadly reverberations building, building . . . then quieting with each second that passed. The thrashing did the same, until the rumble was little more than a distant thunderclap. Then stillness.

My eyes opened. It was dark as sin's storeroom. In the time it takes to pull in a breath, that mass of sound had become a mass of something that covered me. It caked and packed tight about me.

That's when I recognized it for what it was—a snow slide. I should have known the possibility had lurked above me all day, like a starving wolf on the track of a dull-witted rabbit. I had no time to shout, no time to breathe, no time to do anything save for wake too late. Not that I could have done a thing about it. I should have pressed on when I'd had the opportunity.

Oddly enough, I felt more awake than I had in two days. My

head was clear, my thoughts quick. Then I tried to open my mouth. My bottom jaw barely moved—my mouth was packed with snow crystals like thick, wet sand. I tried to flex my nostrils, to draw in air, but nothing moved. My eyes, open to the snow, stared unblinking, burning with the cold, gritty texture.

Hurry, I told myself. You do not want to die, not on this mountainside, buried until spring. I imagined parts of me jutting skyward, crows and coyotes and famished grizzlies nibbling and gnawing away until I was little more than a scrap of cloth and a boot sole puckering in next year's summer sun.

These maudlin thoughts came to me with finger-snap speed. Despite their urgency I could do nothing to save myself except panic and die, breathless and unmoving. Eyes wide but seeing nothing, the only sense left to me was the feeling of cold and pressure from all around, as if the mountainside itself wanted to squeeze me into something so small I might never be found. Ah well, I thought, at least that would foil the critters looking for an easy meal.

Then the feeling of pressure was interrupted by another feeling, of something touching me. Down low, beside my boot, then along my boot and up my leg, an irregular but steady thumping, as if I were being pawed and dug at by . . . something. Something that shifted the snow beside me.

It felt as though a cavity in the snow had opened up. I moved my leg a little bit, then the cavity widened, and I felt like it was traveling up the side of me. Again, I shifted my leg, and the opening that was forming moved back. Hot pain stung me. I was glad to feel something, but this soon felt wrong. Was it a beast? That did not seem possible.

Whatever it was kept clawing and biting and tearing. Soon it reached my side and dug at my right arm, using it for traction as it thrashed. I heard something. Or perhaps I felt it, like a vibration of noise, a low grumble. I thrashed against it, whatever it was, being my only chance to live through this living burial. I was gashed, bitten, clawed for my efforts. And the rumbling, grumbling, snarling drew closer, using me as something to climb.

Despite the snow packing my nose, I swear I smelled something awful. A stink of fetid meat, of animal musk, of rank, raw beast.

From the moment I awoke, already pummeled and sealed tight in my snowy tomb, until the thing clawed its way up me, then burst outward with a guttural hissing growl, less than a half-minute had passed. It felt like two days.

Whatever it was had carved away enough of the rock-hard snow up my side, then along my neck, that I was able to shift my head to my right, retching and coughing and snotting in a spray of snow and blood. As soon as air could pass into me, I gasped, sucking it in, overwhelming my nostrils and throat. I coughed and gagged and little by little I was able to breathe, all the while clawing with my right hand's fingers until I could raise it enough to clear the snowpack from before my chest.

Long minutes passed as I dug and wriggled and thrashed. I am not too proud to admit I panicked several times in the process, so tightly packed did I feel. Only by calming myself, forcing my breathing to smooth out, was I able to extricate myself from the suffocating stonelike hole in which I found myself.

I finally was able to claw my right arm back and forth, raking snow downward into the beast's channel. I pictured my arm as a creature of its own, making slow progress, as if it were taking tiny steps, one, pull . . . two, pull . . . three, then rest, gasp, calm down. And again. In the midst of this endeavor, I heard a bestial sound.

There, not a dozen feet away, side-slope of me, hunched a snarling black and silver wolverine, the very devil of the mountains. I'd only seen one from a distance, and always the sight had set my teeth together tight, out of fear, respect, or awe, perhaps all three.

They are fearsome and feared creatures, and for earned reason. No other beast, and none of such modest size, no larger-bodied than a cattle dog, will openly attack a grizzly bear. Perhaps a man would, but then only with a powerful charge of gunpowder, never with naught but tooth and claw.

It regarded me with narrowed eyes dark as black moons, teeth bared, its body haired up and hunched. A low, chesty grumble of rage and annoyance filled the air between me and the brute.

The growl built, unleashed as a bearish, catlike snarl. The beast spun on its sizable hairy paws, scampered and slid cross-slope. It loped down a swell on the smooth snowscape, and was gone, leaving behind a furrow in the snow.

I realized then that my spot for the night had been the entrance to its den, something I'd not seen sign of when I had approached. This bothered me, as it meant I was more fatigued than I knew, to miss something as obvious as a critter's den, something I prefer to give ample berth when traveling. It would not occur to me until later this may have been but one entrance or exit to its lair. I gave the beast no further thought at the time, requiring something far more urgent than answers.

I had air, finally, but needed more. The sudden desperation to be freed from my still-grasping pack of snow overwhelmed me and I bellowed and thrashed. What came out was a grunt and my one loose arm clawed upward through the wolverine's channel. I saw pink dots on the snow, guessed the beast had drawn my blood on the way up, and I didn't care. It had, after all, saved my life. How many folks, I wonder, can say that? Then I realized I was being hasty. I was not dead yet, but neither was I freed from the snowpack.

Inch by frustrating, agonizing inch I clawed my way out of that denseness. It took forever and a day; the entire time a scream of panic and anger boiled up and out of me, such that I had to stop for breath too frequently. I did not want to, but I could not proceed without frequent pause. My aim was to get that one arm, my right, up out of the hole and into the open air. It finally worked.

I have no idea how long I was at it, but the sun was still pinned high in the blue sky, the slope glistened with the false promise of a thousand lifetimes worth of diamonds, and I was still alive.

I took stock of myself as I knelt on the slope, chest working like a bellows, right arm and leg with punctures through my thick layers of coat and woolen longhandles and buckskin. I patted my waist with my left hand. The knife, near as I could feel with my numb fingertips, was still there. I looked down, expecting to see ice-blue fingers. Instead I saw a red limb.

I blinked hard and looked again. It was the sock, Jack's wool sock, still on my left hand like a mitten. The same could not be said of my right.

I leaned over, peeked into the mostly filled-in hole left by my emergence, and saw more red. Blood from my leg and arm, thanks to the wolverine. But the red looked thick down there. I hesitated to lower any part of my body back into that depression, no matter how shallow it now was, but I had to know.

I flexed and found my right hand to be in decent working order. I clawed down in there and yes, it was the other sock. Somehow it had come off in my frenzy. All my dry wood was gone, but my possibles bag was still around my neck, my knife still at my waist, and my hat . . . I patted my head, but it was bare. The snow had dragged that away. With any luck I'd not be here in the spring to find it. Not that it had been much of a hat at the end anyway, scorched and sodden and sagged from all the wetness that melting snow and head heat bring. Still, a man's hat is a man's hat and mine had been with me a long time. I felt a fleeting moment of annoyance at its loss.

CHAPTER TWELVE

As I looked around myself on the sunny, snowy slope, I realized I had two choices. I could turn back or I could keep moving toward the pass. The trip thus far had whittled on me until I felt like a nub of my old self. I was still big and homely, but I was losing weight, I felt weak, and I was addled in the head from the clubbing those bastards gave me on the train. Still, turning back didn't make sense. I'd come this far, the pass was closer than the wreckage of the train, and the girl, Annette, needed my help.

There was also that unspoken allure of the unknown. What lay beyond the pass? I've been through enough mountain passes to know there are more of the same ahead. I'd likely see a downslope leading to yet another mountain valley, more rough country, and then another pass, and another. They would end eventually, but the trick was to guess right, make certain I chose the pass they went through, all the while scratching that itch to see what sat around the next bend.

Mostly it was anger that drove me. The latest was the wolverine. While I was grateful to the beast for saving my hide, as the hours wore on and I trudged side-slope, switchbacking toward the pass, the punctures he'd given me while burrowing out of the snow began to burn and itch.

As such annoyances will do, it took me longer than it should have to work out that I likely had a blood sickness from that critter. I felt hotter and slower-witted as the day wore on, but kept telling myself it was the day's sun and my lack of food.

Water I had, in the form of snow, and I did my best to shovel it in as I walked. Sometimes I pretended it was mashed potatoes, chunky with thick beef gravy and peppered nicely on top. Sometimes it would be dumplings atop a bowl brimming with bubbling venison stew, carrots and potatoes and onions cut thick and competing with cubes of delicate meat. Mostly it did not work. Stew is stew and coffee is coffee and snow, in the end, no matter how convincing a fellow might be to himself, is only snow.

Long before I wanted it to, the sun dipped behind the largest peak to my left, the west, leaving me in shadow. The air, which moments before had been bright and warm, now hung cold and still. Sound dulled, too, the closer I drew to the pass.

I am not certain when I noticed the snow had tapered to ragged dregs of slushy melt, ridged in spots where the sun would have to work harder to chew it away. When I was within fifty yards of the base of the cleft, I became aware that I was walking on more gravel than snow. I heard the dull crunch and slide of my boots as I dragged, stepped, and wedged them against a slide downhill.

The climb became more strenuous, and keeping my eyes from roving left and right of their own will became a trick I could not master. I heard hard breathing and it took me too long to realize it came from me. I sounded like an ox in its death spasms. But I had my mind set on getting through that pass, if only to get back into the sunshine for a little longer that day. Maybe, I thought, I would find an ideal spot to camp on the other side.

That last fifty feet took everything I had, and that's when it dawned on me I was sicker than I thought. But that spark of promise that everything would be okay once I made it through the pass kept me going. I slid on the scree, slammed down on my slowly mending knee, and gasped at the fresh wash of pain.

But it also helped clear my head long enough for me to see the most welcome sight I'd spied since leaving the train. Inches below my face, which I had nearly driven into the graveled slope, I saw three puckered knobs of horse drops. And a foot beyond in a patch of finer gravel, the curved indent of a shod hoof. They had come this way. Had to be them. Who in the hell else would be up here?

I pushed to my feet, swaying like a soak at the tail end of a three-day binge. Staggering the few remaining yards, I crested the pass and was rewarded with a view of what lay beyond. But I don't recall much more than that. The rock jags to my right blurred upward into a vast patch of blue sky that fast became encircled with a creeping blackness, like stomped river muck sullying a clear stream.

"A storm coming . . ." I muttered. Then the storm dropped its bleak, black mass right on my big, thick head.

CHAPTER THIRTEEN

". . . Boy, I have never seen the like—no, wait, that's not true! Every time I save your carcass, I see it! And every time I vow it'll be the last. But then you stick your sniffer into trouble and ol' Maple Jack has to pull it out, again and again. I vow, boy, don't you take the prize . . ."

The familiar voice drove through the fog in my head like a rock through water—large and loud and sudden. Maple Jack. Must be I'm at his cabin, I thought to myself. Must be we spent too long the night before sampling the jug, as he calls his favorite hobby. I recalled something about a train, a cluster of men, one of them all duded up and smiling. Then a girl, or her eyes, mostly. And the color blue, richer than any sky.

I was trapped in that annoying place between asleep and awake, where dreams feel far too real but won't let you do a thing about them.

Which would explain why my eyes would not do my bidding. I imagine my eyes had that twitchy look, like a dog gets when he's chasing critters in his dreams.

The girl's face came back to me, then an old woman's. She'd been crying, eyes were red and wet.

"Boy?"

Something nudged me, on the face, I think.

"Roamer . . ."

Breath on my face, smelled bad. Tried to turn away from it.

"Roamer!"

The shout forced my eyes open. A great hairy face leered at me from an inch away. I tried to back up, tried to put space between me and it, enough so I could draw my Schofield.

"Boy! You got to calm yourself! You're acting like I'm some sort of phantom."

I squinted. "Jack?" I whispered in a low, hoarse voice.

The great hairy face split apart in the middle. It was a beard. Maple Jack's beard. "You should be so lucky," he said, wagging a finger. "In fact, you are. 'Cause it's me, all right. Maple Jack, in the flesh." He grabbed his paunch and shook it. "Plenty of it!"

"You're . . . chipper."

"You ain't just whistling, boy."

"Where am I?"

He looked up, squinting and visoring his eyes. "Near as I can tell, and I'm pretty good at such things, we are situated on the western edge of a spiny jag in the Bitterroots . . ." He stopped talking and bent low. "In other words, don't fret about it. You get some sleep. Ol' Jack's here now, so there ain't no cause to worry. Plenty of time for catching up when you've rested." He laid the back of an old horned hand on my forehead. I felt the knobby knuckles. "Be a bit before you're well enough to palaver under the power of your full mind."

"The pass . . . I make it through?"

As I drifted away, I heard Jack's voice. "Yep, we're on the good side of things now, boy . . ."

How much time passed before I again awoke I had no notion, but there was Jack. His face hove into view when I opened my mouth. I ran my stick of a tongue along my two dry lips.

" 'Bout time you raised that big shaggy knob you call a head!"

If I had any doubts before, I knew by now it was Jack. "Good to see you, too, Jack." He was about to launch into a windy tirade. I cut in while I had the chance. "Water?"

"Oh, yeah. Course you'd be thirsty, now wouldn't you?" He brought a tin cup of water to me.

I propped myself up on an elbow and wobbled, so he muckled onto my shoulder to steady me. I drank it down and put away two more before Jack said I should ease off. I don't argue with the man when it comes to tending the afflicted—whatever my affliction was. My mind was still fuzzy around the edges.

"Well now," he said, seating himself cross-legged beside me.

I noticed he had a nice little cookfire crackling behind him. I also noticed a smell, succulent. Some sort of meat bubbling in a pot. The man can make a squirrel with hydrophoby downright tasty. I don't know how he does it. I also got the scent of . . .

"Jack, is that coffee?"

He laughed. "I put that pot on once I figured you'd had all the sleep you needed. For the time being, anyway. Figured if the smell of roasting coffee didn't bring you around, nothing would." He filled the cup from where he was sitting and handed it over. "Hot now, go easy."

I nodded, sipped, and winced as the bold brew burned my tongue. And I didn't care one whit. Never has a cup of coffee tasted so good to a man.

"Told you." He poured himself a cup and blew across the top.

Jack likes coffee but he's not enough of a devotee to risk blisters. I am.

"Jack, I am pleased to see you here. But how did you . . . ?"

He held up a hand, shaking his head. "Why don't you let me do the talking, you lay back and rest up."

A sudden thought jerked me to a sitting position. "But . . . there's a girl, Jack . . ."

To my surprise he laughed, nearly a belly roller. "Always is, ain't there? See here," he pushed a hand against my chest, forcing me to lay back down. "Like I said, let me do the talking for

93

a spell. Not like I don't have practice doing such." He sipped his coffee, his bushy eyebrows raised over the rim as he watched me.

"Okay," I said. "But I don't have a lot of time."

"I might know more than you think I do. So leave off the fretting and let me get on with it, will you?" He smoothed the sleeves on his winter buckskin tunic. He always does that when he's about to embark on a "windy," as he calls his one-sided discourses. I have been around him for years and knew there was no heading him off once he smoothed his sleeves. I settled back and waited, curious that he wasn't concerned that I was concerned, if that makes sense. Heck, I'm beginning to sound like him. That in itself is worrisome.

"When you was late, make that when that contraption you was riding on was late, I decided to sniff around, see what happened to you. Figured it was the blizzard, sure enough." He leaned forward. "Know how I knowed?" He smiled and tapped his nose. "On the second day I smelled smoke from the west. Not regular smoke, though. Odd smoke, like from a . . . oh, I don't know," he pooched his lips and looked at the afternoon sky.

"Maybe from a train wreck?" I said, knowing his game.

He snapped a finger, pointing at me. "You may be right at that. Don't ask me how I know, I just know. But never let it be said I ain't got a sniffer for trouble." He leaned forward. "Unlike some folks, I know when to keep my sniffer out of it." He nodded at me, sipping his coffee.

I could hardly disagree, but I wanted him to get on with his story so I could get to mine. "So you smelled smoke . . . ?"

"Don't rush me, boy. You rush a cake and you'll get a pan full of nothing. And a empty gut, too. Now, where was I? Oh yes, the smoke. So I paid a visit to the railroad boys. Told them that foul contraption of yours is a day late. What you gonna do about it? You know what those useless coin-counting bastards said? They told me since the departure date in Oregon was a day or so either way, they said they'd give it another day or two before they were 'legally obliged to be worried'—I kid you not, those were the words they used!"

Maple Jack was in high dudgeon now; he stood, smoothed his sleeves again, stomped around the campsite, toed a stack of firewood out of his way, then bent to straighten it. All at once he walked back over and plunked down before me again.

"So I washed my hands of those useless town-dwellers, and we headed west. Wasn't more than a day I saw black smoke in the distance, ahead of me, the same smoke I'd been whiffing since leaving that den of fools. Did I mention I have a sensitive sniffer?"

I nodded, but kept myself from pointing out he'd said so at least a hundred times in the last ten minutes.

"I would have made better time, but that overgrown show goat you ride is not impressive in the snow."

I looked over to where Tiny Boy was hobbled, cropping knobs of spiky brown grass. He looked prime, better fed than me.

"You'd think with legs that long he'd be less of a fancy-foot, but no, he acted as if he was too good for walking in snow. But Ol' Mossback, well, he was bred for this, that's what makes us such good companions. We're both like lynxes in the snow, sure-footed and uncomplaining."

Now, I won't argue much about Jack's ability to stay upright even when he's spent too much time with his jug. But uncomplaining? The man will complain because there's nothing to complain about.

"The train, Jack. Did you find it?"

"I did," he said, nodding.

He looked more serious than I'd seen him since I awoke. I

almost hated to ask my next question, but I had to know. "They all okay?"

He nodded. "For the most part, yep. All alive, at least I didn't see sign of anything otherwise. Might be they took to eating on one another before I got there." He winked, but saw it wasn't a comment I found much humor in.

"How many?"

"Oh, let's see. There was a dandy man—couldn't take him at all, he was that annoying. There was a couple of middle-aged women, too. One was on the beefy side, and homelier than a sack of rocks. But a nice thing. She had herself a little Mexican-looking boy. Quiet, but a smart child, I could tell. Had himself bright eyes. Ah, now, who else?"

Jack tapped his forehead, brightening. "There was a little fat man with a bandaged head."

He must have meant the chubby man who looked like a merchant. Too bad it hadn't been the dandy who'd taken a knock to the head.

"Didn't say much, looked to be groggy. I don't know about his odds, I seen that glassy look before and it usually means a life of confusion and misery for whoever has to tend him. Pray he has someone who loves him. Now that I think on it, that homely, big-chested gal was doting on him regular. Might be as well for both of them."

"Jack," I said. "Never have I met a person who can be so cutting and charitable at the same time."

"I will take that as a compliment, though I know half of it wasn't meant as such."

"What about the older woman?"

"Older woman? Why, I clearly recall telling you there was two middle-aged ladies, didn't I?" He had tucked his chin back so his beard flattened against his buckskin. He eyed me as if I had told him his liquor was all gone.

"No, this one was an older lady, white hair pulled back and knotted behind her head. Wore a black dress, light blue eyes. She was distressed."

"That's the other one," he said.

"Hardly middle-aged," I said, then bit my tongue—too late.

"Why, you whelp! That's the trouble with folks younger than they ought to be. No respect for anything other than themselves."

"Pardon me, Jack. I see you've taken a shine to her."

"A shine?" He tried to fix me with a killing stare, but too much red had crawled up his cheeks to make the look dangerous.

Then he switched the subject. "Those folks were nigh on useless. I set off on a hunt for them, which shaved more time off my tracking you. Lucky enough, I found a cow elk foundered in a drift not but a mile from the train. She was near played out. I'll wager the meat wasn't prime, but if I hadn't taken her, the wolves would. I dragged it back and do you know what? Not a one of them had a clue how to dress her out. So I had to tuck in, do the job myself. Then the pretty lady, the one who ain't nowhere near the age you think, she's the only one who lent a hand." He smiled and nodded, as if agreeing with himself.

"By the end she was skinning as if she'd been born to the task. That dandy, though. Turned all green on seeing the bloody snow. Said it was barbaric and gruesome. Can you believe that? So I told him he could gnaw on a strip of charred planking whilst the rest of us had elk steaks. Once that meat commenced to sizzle and pop on the flame, that little bastard changed his tune."

"Then you came after me."

"I'm getting to that! Now, where was I? Yes, that fine woman filled me in. Told me all about the rogues who robbed the train and killed the engineers. The passengers did their best for those boys, by the way. Wrapped 'em in makeshift winding sheets and set them back inside the engine where the critters couldn't get at them. I set off trailing you. I figured you'd either be alive or dead, either way I'd find you."

"Glad it's the former, Jack."

Jack nodded, then looked at his stew. "That's about ready. I expect you're hungry. After we eat you can fill me in on your escapades. From the looks of your trail, I'd say you had plenty of fun."

I sat up straighter and tried not to wince at the various scratches and punctures up my right side. That wolverine had sunk fang and claw more than a couple times in me.

We ate the first bowl full in silence, each dwelling on our own thoughts. Finally Jack set down his dish, smoothed his moustaches, and said, "Warned you about them trains, didn't I? They ain't natural. All these newfangled contraptions nowadays, why look at the filth they spout! Like a dragon from tales of yore!"

"Tales of yore?" I said. Jack has a tendency when he's worked up about something to slip into grand speech. "You been reading books again?" I looked toward the sunset to hide my grin. It didn't diminish Jack's roosterish rage. I should have known better.

CHAPTER FOURTEEN

"You mean to tell me you were holed up with a wolverine?" The look Jack gave me was one I'd never seen on his face in all the years I've known him. "That's either the tallest windy anyone's ever told," he said. "Or it's the boldest experience anyone's ever lived through!"

I couldn't help feeling pleased. It's not often I'm able to render Maple Jack close to speechless. I wanted to enjoy the moment, as it might be a long time before it happened again.

"How about I tell you the rest from the trail?"

He shook his head, dismissing the thought as if he'd been waiting for me to ask it. Likely he had. "Be dark in less than two hours. Besides, you're not well enough to get along. No, tomorrow morning's soon enough."

"But," I said, pushing myself up to a sitting position. "The girl is counting on me."

"That's right she is. And if you set off half-cocked, you'll be useless to her. Best get rest whilst you can, boy. Besides, and you won't want to hear this, anything that's been done to that girl has been done already."

"What if they won't keep her around?"

He nodded. "It's a risk, but so is traveling down this mountainside at night, leading Ol' Mossy, with you, half-dozing in your saddle on that big feed-eater you ride."

I knew he was right, I did not feel much like riding, and not in the dark.

Jack ran his fingertips through his bushy beard. He'd begun work on it, as he says, in August, in preparation for the coming cold months. All that means is he stopped trimming it. Come February, he'll look like a silver-topped, shaggy-headed beast, half man and half bear. Right then, he still looked somewhat approachable, almost as if he could visit a town and not cause too much of a ruckus.

Though he avoided clusters of population such as towns, or anything larger than a dug-out trading post, his definition of a populated place is suspect and extreme, even for me. I reckon I've not helped in that regard, as he's come to rely on me to ferry various goods to him from town. The man likes a steady supply of flour, cornmeal, dried beans, spices, tobacco for his pipe, and coffee for his battered old trail pot. Mostly, Jack likes his whiskey. Or as he calls it, his "medicinals."

I don't mind. I can never repay him for all the kindnesses he's shown me over the years, the first and not the least was saving my life in the midst of a blizzard when I was but an overgrown boy wandering on my own in the wildlands of the West.

Little has changed, except now I'm older, and though I spend much of my time alone, I have a friend, and that counts for a whole lot these days.

"You going to laze all day or are you going to tell me about this so-called wolverine?"

"How do you explain these?" I said, raising my arm to indicate the muslin-wrapped spots where he'd applied one of his foul-smelling but effective poultices. This was a particularly rank batch, the stink of which put me in mind of a skunk's trail leavings mixed with scrapings of greened venison.

Jack was forever learning new remedies from his Indian friends. This one, he said, came from the Salish. I think he secretly likes it when I show up with some ailment or other.

Gives him the opportunity to test his latest potions, what he calls his magical cures. I am still alive despite or because of them, so who am I to argue?

"Now I come to think on it, it might explain those holes something put in you." He leaned forward. "You certain it wasn't a rabbit? Maybe a porcupine?"

I leaned back and told him the story. Every so often he would nod or grunt. I told him of my first night under the tree.

"Yep, I crawled in there, saw your sign. Figured it had to be you, no other critter that big would still be roving these heights, too dumb to hibernate." He winked and topped off our cups of coffee, dolloping in a couple of swallows each from a bottle of "tonic" that tasted an awful lot like whiskey.

I told him about the foolishness in settling in for the night in that rocky spot, the den that looked too good to be true. And then the avalanche, the horror of being under all that snow. That nightmare feeling rippled through me again as I told him.

"I found a man once," said Jack. "It was in the springtime, years back, along a splinter range up in the territories. I was packing in goods for a family of missionaries—that's a whole other tale, oddballs ain't the word for those thumpers—when I come upon a man's hand stiff and curled like a claw, jutting right outta the snow. Like this!" He held up his arm, his fingers curled as if he were holding a rock the size of a cat's head. No one tells a story like ol' Jack.

He'd paused, holding that claw of a hand on high as if he were displaying a prize. I asked what that hand in the snow had to do with what I'd been telling him.

"Should think that'd be obvious. Honestly, boy, sometimes you worry me. A barnyard goose could have made the connection betwixt the stories. The man I found had been laid low by a snow slide. You're lucky that knob of boulders was there, elsewise you'd have been smeared all over that slope."

"So you think my bunking in with the wolverine proved a good choice, then."

Jack wrinkled his nose and squinted at me. "Now I didn't say that. Go to sleep before you tell me something you'll regret."

A few minutes later, when we were both in our blankets, I said, "Jack?"

"Yep."

"How was the girl's aunt?"

"She's a tough chicken, no doubt."

"I know, but . . ."

"Be good to find the girl, Roamer. Her aunt ain't so tough she won't break apart if we don't."

"First thing, then?"

Jack sighed. "Only if you quit your yammering. I require a full night's sleep or I'm liable to be surly come tomorrow."

"You could sleep for a month and you'd still be surly." I slipped into slumber, a smile on my face, listening to the sound of Maple Jack muttering.

CHAPTER FIFTEEN

As I expected, we were up early. I made coffee while Jack broke camp all around me. "Never saw a grown man so fond of a drink as you are of that coffee. My word, anybody'd think you were suckling on the titty the way you work that cup."

"I could say the same about someone I know and his jug of firewater. But I won't stoop so low as that. No sir," I said, not daring to look at Jack for fear I'd start laughing. "I won't do it."

Jack reddened, then mumbled as he finished lashing together what remained of the firewood he'd gathered. He snugged it lengthwise atop the panniers and turned to saddle Tiny Boy.

"I can do that, Jack. You've done more than your share. I'm fine."

"Time will tell, Roamer. All the same, you best ride awhile. Make this hayburner earn his keep." He ran a knobby hand along Tiny Boy's thick neck. The big horse nuzzled Jack's shoulder. As I suspected, the old mountain man had taken exceptional care of my trail mate and I was glad of it.

I finished saddling the horse, then tied on my gear in two canvas sacks draped behind the cantle. Jack had kindly lugged all my gear with him, lashed atop Tiny Boy. What gear I lacked, which had burned in the passenger car, Jack provided out of his own stores.

The last thing we did was drain the remaining coffee into our waiting cups, then cool off and rinse out the pot in a lingering berm of slushy snow. I used the pot to ferry snow onto the already doused campfire. I've never seen any good come from treating a campfire with laziness. Slumbering coals have a knack for waking, and their bite can be deep and deadly.

When no ready water source or snowpack is nearby, a favorite trick of the woodsman is to make water on the fire's remains. Nothing like the steaming hiss of a dying fire to let a man know he's done the job.

I managed to hoist myself up into the saddle while Jack yellowed the snow atop the fire. "Good and dead," he said, lacing up his buckskins and tugging on Mossy's reins. "Now let's cover ground."

It was still early. Gray light from the east had begun rising over the ridge behind us, the pass no longer visible. Jack had somehow managed to drag my burly self a goodly ways down the mountainside before he'd set up our camp.

Close to two hours later we heard the beast. I should say Tiny Boy, whose hearing is acute and uncanny in its power of long-distance perception—could be I am biased—heard the beast, and well before we saw it. By the time Ol' Mossback heard it, Tiny had nickered low and shook his head, ears swiveling and nostrils flared in agitation. Mossy let out his own reaction—a braying sound that takes some getting used to. Truth is, it sounds like a long-abused wheel axle in sore need of grease.

We paused, Jack cupped a hand around an ear. I sat up taller in the saddle, the leather creaking. There it was again, faint but steady. A moaning sound both ominous and chilling.

"What on earth . . ." Jack leaned forward, as if to hear it better.

"Doesn't sound normal." I slid down from Tiny Boy, as I'd done several times already that day to give him a rest and stretch my stiffening muscles. I winced but less so than earlier.

Unspeaking, we moved forward, each of us leading our mounts. We'd long since switchbacked our way downslope, well below treeline. The flora here was less stunted and not far below I saw wind-rustled spruce branches. I also thought I caught the sun's momentary glint off a thin curving thread of a stream. That promised a decent campsite for the evening, though I knew we needed to speed our progress toward the girl. My heart was willing, but my body was another matter. Such thoughts angered me and I squashed them even as they popped up in my mind like prairie dogs.

Jack led the way, arcing wide to the south with the intention of coming upon the source of the sounds from an angle of advantage rather than from above, a direction we'd be harder-pressed to defend. The closer we drew to the thing making the sound, the more agitated Mossy and Tiny Boy became, whickering low and twitching their ears.

Jack slid his old cap-and-ball war cannon free from the waist sash he kept it tucked under and I did the same with the backup revolver in my saddlebag. It was a long-barrel Colt I'd taken from a man who'd threatened to kill me with it a long time ago.

Jack nodded to me, cutting his eyes to Tiny as he looped Mossback's reins around a stout jut of stone. He cinched them tight and double-tied them. I did the same with my reins. Past experience is a harsh master. Spooked steeds will bolt and chasing them down is rarely enjoyable.

We low-walked toward the moaning sound and Jack bent, parting branches with the barrel of his old pistol. I looked over his shoulder.

In the midst of a small clearing, no larger than a buckboard, a black horse, stripped of tack, lay on its right side, stretched out as long as a horse can get. Its back arched into irregular spasms, bending the spine into an impossible crescent before relenting.

Plainly a mare, the beast twitched its rearmost hooves, closest to us, as if trying to propel itself forward. The earth beneath her was churned to muck and the horse had fouled itself as much as it would ever be able to, its leavings smeared about its flanks had somewhat dried.

A raw, animal scent met our noses, a stink of filth and fear. Grunts punctuated the steady groaning.

"Indian?" I said in a whisper, knowing the answer.

"Not likely," said Jack. "She's shod, but . . ." His voice trailed off.

I saw no sign of anyone else around. From the looks of the site, she'd thrashed for quite some time, though from our position there was no clear reason why. Her groans and harsh, stuttery breaths got to me. I pushed past Jack, my gun out, somehow knowing no one else was around.

"Boy!" said Jack, but he, too, came out of hiding.

"Keep an eye," I said and knelt to the beast. If she was aware of our presence, she didn't show it. Her long nose was a smear of cuts, blood, bubbled saliva, and muck from the recent melt. I laid a hand between her eyes. She neither slowed her grunting and hoarse breaths nor flickered an open eyelid at the touch of my hand. Her upturned eye bulged. The veins around the center had popped and looked like poorly rendered lines on a hasty map.

"Here's the trouble," said Jack, bending down and lightly touching a finger to her leg. I'd not seen it until then. Her right front leg was broken, splintered enough between the knee and hock that a jag of bone jutted through a gash. The wound was not fresh, and though smeared with muck, continued to ooze blood and pus. The swelling at the joints made me wince even more than seeing the bone.

A horse with a broken leg is no use to anyone, especially not itself. Anyone with a fleck of sympathy in their soul will put down such a beast as a kindness before the agonies of long suffering wash over it. Jack read my mind.

"Someone . . . some bastard . . . did this. Rode her down in this hard place, stripped her clean, then left her to die." He stood, his cheek muscles bunched tight beneath his beard. His face shook with ill-controlled rage.

"Only she didn't die."

"Stand back, son." He thumbed the hammer on his gun.

I laid a hand on his arm. "Sound carries," I said, looking him in the eye.

"You rather cut her throat? Bleed her out? Hasn't she suffered enough?"

I swallowed, torn for the briefest of moments, wondering if our quarry would hear it. I shook my head. "You're right, but I'll do it, Jack. You don't have to," I cocked my revolver, looking at him.

He closed his eyes, nodded, then turned away. Jack can seem a hard character, but he's the kindest man I've ever met. Beasts would say the same thing if they could.

I bent and set the snout of the gun in the sunken spot above her twitching eye. "I'm sorry, girl," I whispered. "It will be better soon." I looked away, touched the trigger, and felt the tool do its job.

A tight, small clot of sound burst deep in her throat. She stiffened once more, her full length, then a low groan, her last ever, leaked from her mouth, tapering to silence. I thumbed her eyelid down over that staring eye. Another futile human gesture, I reckon. But it was all I could do, the least I could do.

At that sad moment, I only wanted to throw the Colt as far as I could. It was not the gun's fault, I know, and they are among the most useful of tools, especially to a man who must defend himself and provide for himself and others. But I dislike their sudden finality. Would that happiness in life came about as quick and bold.

We stood in silence, staring down at the once-beautiful

creature. Finally, Jack spoke.

"How long?" His voice was thick.

"Days," I said, surveying the dismal place.

"Didn't tell me we were dealing with the lowest of the low, boy. Any man who will treat a workmate in such a hard manner don't deserve a thing but payment in kind."

I couldn't disagree.

He jerked his chin upslope. "That's where she likely lost her footing." I followed his gaze to a couple of rough furrows plowed in the scree-pocked soil. A sapling lay snapped nearby. Jack stalked the clearing, cutting wide around the dead horse.

"Mmm," he grunted, toed dirt with his moccasin. "Rider was throwed, fell hard. Dug with his hands here, looks like claw marks, maybe from pain. Good. Serves the killer right. Hope he's carrying a frightful affliction. Not enough, but it'd be a start."

"You're saying 'he.'"

He nodded. "Yep, 'twas a man. Unless that young lady's wearing a man's boot." He nodded at the ground, nudging a churned spot with his toe.

"We best go," I said. I was already headed back through the trees to Mossback and Tiny Boy. "Get as far as we can before we camp. One good thing—likely someone's riding double. Might slow them a bit. I doubt we can catch them, they've had too good a start, but we can trail them right to the ocean if need be."

From behind me I heard Jack. "And then some," he said. The grim set of his jaw and his cold, hard eyes told me he wasn't kidding.

CHAPTER SIXTEEN

"You know, Jack, I never cease to be amazed at your speed when you're on a mission." And I meant it, too. We were camped once more, but he'd hoofed it hard all afternoon in hopes of gaining on the killers. I should have left it at that, but I pressed on. "In fact, for an old man, you move like a mountain tiger when the urge takes you."

I made damn certain I was out of swinging range when I said it. It was a risky pair of bold statements, but I had to do something to break the mood we'd been traveling under since we'd left the poor horse behind hours before. At least her carcass would feed wolves, coyotes, wolverines, and lord knows what else.

Although I know flattery is one of Maple Jack's weaknesses, I also know he's dumb like a fox and knows a jibe when he hears it. Jack surprised me by smiling, even as his neck blossomed red as he hunched over the fire stirring the bubbling stew. I knew better. I'd stung him, maybe too hard with the old man dig, but he was forever needling me about my size. It was all in good faith, to be sure, but not something I can help any more than he can being older than me.

Jack straightened, made a show of stretching his back, then spun on the balls of his feet, set to dive for me. Lucky for me, he caught his right heel on a rock and flopped backward, square in the dirt on his backside.

I tamped down the urge to give him a hand up, which I knew

he'd refuse. Mood he was in, he might snap at me like an angry dog. I kept my seat, arched an eyebrow, and poked the needle through the hide of my buckskin shirt with my leather thumb patch. That gave me one more stitch closer to cinching up the various rips and claw holes and tooth snags and burns I'd endured over the past few days. It felt like a month.

I couldn't help myself and I opened my mouth yet again, suppressing a smile. "Well that proves it . . . grace and speed are two different things."

"I've had enough of you and your palaver." Jack managed to grunt to his feet and wagged the dripping stirring stick at me. "You call me a fat old man one more time and you'll see what this fat old man can do!"

"Well now," I finished tugging the waxed thread tight. I set it aside and wiped from my forehead the tepid drops of stew he'd flecked at me. I licked my fingertip. "Could use more salt."

Even in the low glow from the fire, I saw my friend's nostrils flare and his eyes squint.

I wasn't quite done. "And I never said you were fat. But now that you bring it up . . ."

That time, I was on my feet and giggling like an overtired child as Jack chased me around the fire, swinging his stew stick and cursing me with words I don't believe have ever been uttered by humans.

"I been thinking on it and I do believe I know where those rascals are headed."

We'd both been walking, me in front, leading Tiny Boy, Jack and Mossy behind. We were hoofing it, not dawdling, but neither of us like to ride our beasts for long; somehow it doesn't set well. Bad enough to load Tiny with all manner of goods I'm carrying, though I try to keep my pile of possessions to a minimum.

I can't say the same for Jack. That man likes to acquire things, even if it's a funny-looking stick he says he's going to whittle on. I haven't seen him whittle more than five minutes at a stretch, but I guess Ol' Mossback is used to the man's ways, for he doesn't kick up a fuss. Well, not regularly.

"Where's that, then?" I said, not daring to slow or stop, because Jack would take that as an invitation to set up camp and make a feed. I didn't want to take the time. That girl was getting farther from me with every slow step I took. So I made damn sure I took faster steps.

"A mountain town, ghost town now. Folks who lived there called it a city, though that is stretching things a bit. Ain't no more a city than my cabin is a bustling seaport."

"You've been to it before?"

"Yep," he said, angling up beside me at the top of yet another small rise.

Below us, a long, narrow mountain valley spread its arms wide in the day's cold temperature.

"But that was a long time ago," he said. "Nigh on twenty years, more or less, if I had to guess."

"How far?"

"Oh," Jack offered up a yawn, "ain't that far now." He nodded downslope.

At first I didn't see anything but the lodgepole pines studding the hillside. And then I saw the telltale signs of a place once occupied by humans, though now it bore the distinct look of dereliction.

CHAPTER SEVENTEEN

If anyone still lived here, I'd be mighty surprised. From the look of it, this town had long since withered on whatever vine had at one time gumption enough to set a root here. As if reading my mind, Jack sidled close. I looked down at him. Not like the man to stand so close to anyone, except perhaps to his winter woman, but I hadn't actually ever met her.

In a low voice, he said, "Sound carries." He jerked his beard downslope toward the scatter of buildings. "As I said, I been here before. Some time ago, though. Didn't look nothing like this. It was full of people. And kids, too."

I tamped down a grin. Wouldn't do to have Jack think I took issue with the fact he doesn't consider children as people. Didn't work, he saw me smirk.

"You whelp, I'm trying to educate you on this situation and you're acting like a child."

"You're right, sorry. I guess the gold ran out, huh?" I scanned the vista below, seeing more remnants of buildings the more I looked. Gray-boarded shacks leaned against trees, others now little more than piles of puckered planks; here and there bones of rusted sluices were visible. One jutting piece of tin wagged in a breeze, as yet unfelt by us. It gave off a slight squeak that sounded like a donkey heard from afar.

"Was a hell of a place at one time. But it's not what you think. No gold here. Oh, I'm sure they all tried to pan for it at one time or another. But it was sapphires that occupied their time."

"Sapphires?"

"Yep, and they were the prettiest blue stones you ever did see. Was a time when it looked like the river would never run out of them. Town was a booming place. Had more money and more robberies than a town this size ought. Yes sir, all manner of craziness went on here."

"I never would have guessed they'd find precious stones all the way up in the hills like this."

"Well, they did, and that's a fact." Jack nodded, lost in thought as he gazed down the valley.

"I assume the stones did run out then."

"In a manner of speaking, yes." He looked at me. "Same old story. Greed. It got the best of them. Like the old tale about the man who had a goose that laid golden eggs. That was a pretty good deal for him. Then after a fashion, one egg at a time wasn't enough. He wanted more and more. Finally he got so tired of waiting, he up and killed that bird, figured he'd get at all the eggs at once."

I nodded, familiar with the story. "Only it didn't work out that way."

"No sir, it did not. He ended up with a stringy old bird in the stewpot and no more eggs forever."

"So you're saying they killed the source of their sapphires?" I was a little confused, a whole lot curious.

He nodded. "I wasn't here at the time, but I heard about it years later."

"How'd they do it?"

"Bunch of those idiots got together, decided they could get a leg up on their wealth faster by blasting at the source of their bountiful creek."

"They didn't."

"Yep, sure did." Jack offered a rueful grin. "A dumber, greedier bunch of fools you'd be hard-pressed to find gathered in one place. Except in Washington, D.C."

"So that's why I don't see a creek down there. Naught but a snaky trail where one might have been."

Jack nodded. "They stuffed the mouth of that creek where it bubbled out of the mountainside with nitro and a few kegs of gunpowder for good measure. Made a hell of a racket, brought down half the hillside, buried a handful of houses, a couple of dumb miners, and worst of all . . ."

"Diverted their creek," I said.

Jack nudged me with an elbow. "You ain't so thick as you look, boy. Don't care what everyone else says." He winked to let me know I was being funned, as he calls it. I had it coming.

"No idea where that flowage went," he said. "Tucked itself down deep underground, I expect, only to come out someplace else. Maybe where it would be respected more than yonder. Wherever it was, it was far enough away that the town dried up. No water, no town. Heard from an old mountain goat friend of mine that the place looks like everybody got up one day from their tables and chairs and walked on out their doors, didn't look back. Left their clothes, food, tools, the lot. Up and walked away."

"What would make them do that? Surely not just the water."

Jack shrugged, looking at me askance. "Some say those fools unleashed a mountain spirit that day they blasted the river." He tapped a grimy finger to the side of his nose and nodded.

I smiled. "So it was an irate spirit that drove them out of town. Right in the middle of a meal."

Jack shrugged again. "Just because you don't believe in a thing, boy, don't mean you have the right to go poking and prodding and making fun of it."

We stood in quiet for a moment. Around us, a light afternoon breeze soughed through pine branches, wagging them before moving on.

"What was this place called?"

"Take a guess," said Jack, grinning.

I shrugged. "Dream's End?"

He looked at me, his head pulled back as if I'd sworn in church. "You are a gloomy Gus. No, they called it Sapphire City, of course."

"Of course," I said. "Funny what greed will do to a person." I said it, but I couldn't help myself. My eyes narrowed and I looked toward the old stream bed. Makes a man wonder. Maybe the urge to procure shiny, fancy things of no practical worth is a basic human instinct. I wish I was above such distractions, but I reckon I will never be. As long as I'm alive, I'll be forever swayed by a bauble, a flash of prettiness.

Takes a whole lot to overlook beauty and move on. And I don't care what anyone says, even if you do move along, you are forever changed by your exposure to beauty. You're never the same man again. My thoughts turned to the girl in blue. I hoped she was still alive, still as dignified as she seemed on the train, and hope of hopes, that she was being treated better than I suspected she was.

"Roamer, where are you now, boy?" Jack looked up at me, a half-smile on his face. "You got that dazed thinkin' look of yours." He walked away, scratching his neck. "I swear, you'll get on one of those thinking jags of yours one of these days and blump! You'll drop right down an old mine shaft. Last thing any of us hear will be your big carcass whistling on down in the dark, bouncing off rocks and shoring timbers, before a godawful crash when you hit bottom. And that, my friend, will be that."

He winked again. "Come on, back away from here. We'll camp down that gully we climbed up out of. That way we can have ourselves a fire to enjoy whilst we take turns keeping watch.

I don't trust those rascals."

"Jack, we have to get down there. We made it this far, there's no telling if they're even there."

"I know, I know, but I have to have a bite of food. We don't fortify ourselves, we'll be as sad as a pair of hounds on dog-washing day."

"Grab some jerky and let's go. We wasted enough time getting here."

"You get any bossier with me and you can go on down there alone. Me, I'm having a meal."

"Fine," I said, rummaging in my bag for more ammunition for the Colt. "Enjoy yourself. I'll be back in a bit. I want to scout the place. For all we know they've been here and gone for a day or longer. The sooner we find out, the better off we'll all be."

Jack leaked out a long sigh. I knew I had him. I didn't wait for him, though. He could catch up with me. I set off, keeping low and doing my best not to raise dust. It wasn't so easy and I knew Jack had a point. It wouldn't have been wise if they were down there. It would have been far wiser to trail down under cover of dark.

At least I had trees. Thick stands of lodgepole pines stippled the slope. I made my way northward, trusting the afternoon sun, dipping below the west rim of the narrow mountain valley, casting enough doubting shadows to mask my movements.

I carelessly clunked the toe of my right boot against a loose cobble. I seized in place, as unmoving as a knotted rope. The rock rolled downslope a dozen feet and cracked against a larger jut of granite. It stopped there but the sound, I was convinced, would be louder than a gunshot by the time it echoed down to the town.

"You want to get us both killed, you big oaf?"

I turned my head and there was Jack, not a dozen feet behind me. I'd been so set on not making a sound I hadn't paid attention to anything else, least of all my back trail.

"I thought you'd be halfway through a beefsteak dinner by now, Jack."

"And leave you to get yourself killed or worse? Nah, didn't want that on my conscience. Much noise as you're throwing around, I'd be mighty surprised if they don't open fire on us any time now. Now look, I got a plan. We split up, I'll go yonder." He wagged the barrel of his revolver toward the north side of the row of derelict buildings flanking what I assume had once been Main Street. "One of us is bound to find her. Then we'll meet up back here in a half hour, where it's safe."

"What are you inclined to do if you meet up with any of them?"

"Likely it will be a situation where self-defense will rule the day. So Maple Jack is inclined, if you please, to save his own hide. Shoot first, whine and worry later. Take my advice, boy. Time enough for contemplation once we're safe. They're the lowest of the low, killers, thieves, and kidnappers, lord knows what else they've got up to."

"And then?" I said, amazed at his ability to simplify the diciest of situations.

"Then we skedaddle," he said, winking and pushing past me.

"All that is fine . . . if they're down there."

"Oh, they're down there, all right," said Jack, stopping right in front of me and nodding toward the ghost town.

I followed his sight line and saw movement at the north side of town. A horse walked slowly into view, snorted, and continued circling in a small corral that looked as if it had been hastily resurrected from scraps of planking and poles. I kept watching and in a few moments saw the rump of another horse.

"Somebody's down there, at any rate. Might be our quarry, might be someone else fool enough to be up here in October."

He winked at me. "Nearly as foolish as us. Come on, let's see if we can't get closer."

And that's what we did. It took a solid ten minutes to switchback our way down there until we were at the valley floor, crouched behind what appeared to have once been a shed, or a paltry excuse for a house. It was big enough to hide us, barely. And that's when we heard a man shout.

His shouts drew closer. We froze in place, not daring to glance at each other.

Another voice joined the shouter. Two men. The second voice sounded as if it were begging, trying to explain something. The shouter shut him down.

CHAPTER EIGHTEEN

"That son of a bitch was supposed to be here! And you!" The shouting man, who even at our fair distance looked plenty familiar, poked the recipient of his rage square in the chest with a hard, ramming finger. The man on the receiving end jerked visibly with each jab, and made no move to shove the poker away.

Of greater interest to me were two things: The man being jabbed was larger than the man poking him, which meant he was afraid of the poking man. And the poking man? None other than Fancy Collar from the train. The other man was unfamiliar to me, so he must have been the one who brought the horses and met the rest of them at the train.

I was barely aware I'd begun to stand and was growling low like a caged beast. Jack snagged my arm and jerked me down, back to cover. "Boy, you want to get us kilt before we make our move?"

They hadn't heard us. I settled beside Jack, not an easy thing to do when we were so close to our quarry. I hadn't seen sign of the girl in blue. I knew I couldn't keep still much longer. But I knew, too, that Jack was right—if I acted in haste, we'd both end up leaking out our last right there on the damn half-snowed soil of this hard little valley in the middle of a scatter of mountains that people like these fools have no business being in. And from what Jack had said, that's exactly what I would

119

have told the people who built this sad little wreck of a mine camp.

Fancy Collar resumed his shouting in the larger man's face, who'd hung his head down to oblige the red-faced man. "I said to make sure none of the others touched her, didn't I? Didn't I?"

The bigger man nodded, a glum look tugging his head and shoulders down, as if his head bounced on a string.

"I didn't hear you!"

"I said, 'Yes, boss.' "

"That's right. And to your credit, you did as I asked you. But I failed to point out that that directive also included you. Am I correct?"

"Yes, boss." The bigger man would not raise his eyes from staring at their toe-to-toe boots in the middle of the dusty little street.

"What did I find when I got back from scouting?" Fancy Collar walked in a tight circle, raised his arms, let them drop, then faced the man once more. "I'll tell you what I found. You with your hand down that girl's dress front, and her screaming blue murder! And you laughing about it!"

Fancy Collar's voice had climbed to a screeching shout. Even from our distance I saw the red of his face begin to purple. With no warning he pulled his left leg back and drove the toe of a dusty black boot hard into the big man's shin. Jack and I both winced.

A groan burst from the man's drawn mouth. I almost felt sympathy. He dropped to one knee, wobbled there, wheezing and rubbing his shin. "Jesus, boss—I . . . I said I was sorry."

The next thing we saw was a two-shot derringer, nickel with white pearly grips, gleaming in Fancy Collar's right hand. He cocked it. "Not sorry enough, fool," and before the man could raise his head, Fancy Collar jammed the snout of the gun into the back of his brown hair and touched the trigger.

The little gun popped, the man's eyes pulsed wide like quail eggs, and I swear he looked right at us. His lean face widened, as if inflated for the briefest of moments like a pig's bladder blown up for children to play with. It sunk back in on itself as quickly and a gout of blood erupted between his nose and cheek. He collapsed in an awkward pose, one leg still bent beneath him, as if he had dozed off while genuflecting in church.

"Jackass," said Fancy Collar, a tight sneer pulling his mouth wide. "You brought that on yourself." He spun and stalked away, disappearing behind the nearest in a row of buildings.

I have had the displeasure of killing men, always in defense of myself or others. I have also seen men killed before me. It is never pleasant. Vengeance is not sweet, rage is nothing but foul. They are corrosive and chew away at the killer's core until he, too, even though he may still be afoot, is as dead as those he killed.

My breath came back and I stood, looking at the shot man, then toward where Fancy Collar had gone. "Jack," I whispered, not looking down at my compadre. "See if he's alive. I have to follow that man."

Once more, Maple Jack grabbed my arm, trying to stay my actions. "You'll end up dead or you'll get the girl kilt, or both! We got a plan, Roamer. Stay with it. We'll find her."

I shook my head. "Nope, the time's now, Jack. I've been on this trail far too long. I'll bring her back. You go get the mounts."

He stood. "Like hell."

But I was already moving, following Fancy Collar's trail. I didn't look back at Jack. He'd be steaming angry with me, but I didn't want him to think I was inviting him to come along with me. Truth is, I knew the situation ahead was bound to be as bad as bad can get.

And though Maple Jack is as tough as a handful of hot nails, he has done more than enough on my account over the years. The way I saw it, this was no different, but I had the thin chance of protecting him and I had to grab it. I had to keep him out of harm's way anytime I could. I'd deal with his rage later. If I lived through this mess.

CHAPTER NINETEEN

I kept low and did my best not to step on anything that might snap. That, however, did not happen. I swear my big feet ground more loud gravel than any dozen head of cattle would stomping through the same patch of dirt. Despite the thunder my feet roused, I made it to the safety of the nearest pucker-boarded shack and leaned low and tense, my Colt drawn.

Before I poked my sniffer beyond the edge, I rested my cheek against the sun-warmed board. It felt comforting, I'd say, and the wood still gave off a smell of a forest in autumn. It was a quick, clean moment in what had been a long week of strife and struggle. It isn't over yet, I reminded myself.

I peered around the board, saw nothing, and sucked in a breath. Here we go . . .

I made it along the entire length of Main Street in such a manner. As I stepped, slow and careful, I kept a close eye on as much of what I passed as I was able. A man, should he know he's followed, can conceal himself in most any small, tight space. He can become part of a mere shadow, crouch behind an upended shipping trunk, or spring out from a doorway. None of this happened, which was fine by me. But I did manage to see for myself what Jack's old chum had told him.

Sapphire City had been vacated all right. But it felt as though there was more to the story. Sure the town's water may have dried up, but to leave your cups and plates and spoons and forks on the table? One sideboard still supported a dust-covered

Bible, flayed open, a length of ribbon draped down the center. Coats rode the backs of chairs, hanging as if from bony shoulders of headless men. Bonnets, large and small, hung cheek-to-jowl with straw hats on hooks.

What had happened to make the residents flee in such obvious haste? Could there really be credence in the unleashed mountain spirit story? Like as not, it was Jack spinning a windy for my benefit. Still, something forced these people to leave in one heck of a hurry. It was a mystery, to be certain, one I did not care to dwell on at that moment. Time enough later, to echo Jack's sentiments.

I had to cough, to clear my throat in the worst way, but I did not dare. By my reckoning I was one, maybe two, buildings away from that makeshift horse corral. They had to be encamped nearby. Nobody would stray far from their mounts, especially not in such a mountain-locked place.

The thought occurred to me that's exactly what we had done. Then I had another gut-tightening thought: What if they had known we were tracking them? What if Fancy Collar had sent a man on a wide loop to take us from the rear? Tiny Boy and Mossback would be easy pickings. And then, so would we.

I shook my face. Sweat slid into the corners of my eyes. A droplet made its way down the bridge of my broken nose, bent by fisticuffs with chairs and boards and a couple of lucky punches over the years.

I crouched low, doing my best to cat-foot closer to the corral. One more corner and there it was, a dapple gray horse, not ten feet from me. And it saw me. I pulled back, my lips tight against my teeth. I waited for the beast to nicker. They always do, astute as they are. But no sound came.

Then I heard a voice raised once more in anger. It came from a ways off, farther on down the street. Maybe they hadn't camped close by the horses. Maybe they found the best digs in town, confident that nothing would bother their horses way out here in the midst of little else. I allowed myself a quick flash of hope, and thus emboldened, I bent low and approached the corral.

CHAPTER TWENTY

The shouts increased, two, perhaps three voices, all men, rose and fell, their sharp, barked words distant. I prayed they stayed so. The corral was in full view now. And I counted four horses, none looking particularly healthy. Four would be the correct number, considering it had appeared to me they had put the girl on a horse of her own when I'd seen them riding away from the train that day. That would make five horses. The poor horse on the trail had been ridden hard, broken its leg, and left to suffer. So these four haggard beasts remained.

They seemed tired, though not yet beyond help. I hated to do it, but my plan, meager though it was, required their liberation. As little spunk as they were showing, I wondered if they would indulge me and get very far at all. Not a nicker or whinny from them as yet, just perked ears and curious stares as they milled and regarded me.

I had to try. With one hand I slid the three closest rails out of the rope lashings that held them in place, and swung them wide enough for the horses to pass by and out. I strode into the corral. The nearest horse, a pretty bay mare, rumbled a note of concern and walked in a circle away from me. The corral was not large, perhaps twenty feet across, and with my arms spread wide I was able to roust them into a mild frenzy.

They milled, bumped, and pitched into one another, and finally the first, the pretty bay, with hesitance, stepped past the poles and out into the side street. I offered a couple of low "git up nows" and herded the rest out of there. I was about to step out of the corral myself when a voice from inside the nearest building, what looked to be an old stable, said, "What in the hell?"

I dropped low and froze, but the voice said, "Hey . . . hey it's you!"

And that's all it took. The man cranked back on his gun's hammer and let fly with a bullet intended for me. I kept low and barreled on out of there, keeping the building to my right, looking for the first open doorway.

He hotfooted me up the lane with bullets. My luck held as I saw a parted door sagged in a frame. Couldn't be any worse, so I hit it with a shoulder and the old, dry wood blew apart, splinters and hunks of planking whipping into the dark room. What was left of the door slammed against something and shuddered to a standstill.

The man stopped shooting, but in a way I was happy he had taken shots at me. He spooked the four docile horses. They thundered by as I stomped around in the dark room into which I'd crashed, flailing for my balance.

At least the horses might prove difficult to catch, maybe impossible, with luck. I felt bad about it, forcing them into a short life of misery and death in the mountains, likely to die by fang or claw before the cold and hunger got to them. But life, as I have learned many times through the years, is a constant series of decisions, often an unfortunate one in favor of a choice barely more tolerable.

I heard the man muttering, and didn't know which one of them from the train it was. Sounded like he kicked a board, then I heard his boots stalk away. Anytime now, he would be back with his chums. There should be three in all, Fancy Collar and the two from the train, the fat, ginger-whiskered bald man and Hector.

The fellow who'd been killed had not been on the train. Shouted down, kicked, then shot. Damn hard way to go.

I don't know what I expected to hear, except maybe the voices of those men. Or worse, not hearing them, only the crunch of gravel underfoot, whispered directives. I heard none of it. Three or four quiet minutes passed. Then I heard another quick shout—I couldn't be certain it was Fancy Collar—followed by a gunshot, then another—both sounded like the same gun. Then a third shot boomed out, a different gun—bigger and older, with that boom to it. Not the one I'd had fired at me. Somebody else. There was something familiar about that third shot, but I didn't have time to dwell on it. The shots didn't alarm me as much as what followed tight on their heels: a woman's scream.

There was only one woman I was aware of in Sapphire City. I had to find her. I abandoned the idea of keeping hidden behind buildings as I ran. All that would do is slow me down.

I rounded the last corner to see a scene I did not expect. The lane widened out and sloped downward toward a dry, rocky stretch. Must have been the end of town that bumped up tight to the once-flowing, jewel-filled creek. That would explain the dry, rocky stubble. I'd wager there wasn't a sapphire to be found within a mile radius of the place.

Fancy Collar stood in the center of the wide stretch, the girl beside him. Her big blue eyes were wide, her mouth parted too much by a tight-tied neck scarf, purple in color. That blue cape bore smudges and stains from the trail. Her chest rose and fell quickly, and her arms looked to be tied behind her, hard to tell, the way the cloak hung.

Two prone forms lay at the killer's feet, one I recognized as his henchman, Hector, the drunken man, and the second I saw was Ginger Whiskers. They would account for the first two shots. Hector appeared to still be twitching.

And then I saw why the third shot, the boomer, had sounded

familiar. It had come from Jack's big revolver. And I knew this because my best friend, Maple Jack, was on the ground, hands behind his head, kneeling at the feet of Fancy Collar.

"Go, boy! Go!" shouted Jack. "Do what you need to, don't worry about me—"

Fancy Collar raised his gun, drove it down hard on the top of Jack's pate, snubbing off Jack's words in mid-shout.

"No!" I shouted, barreling forward.

Jack collapsed, his face slamming into the dirt. Dust rose and he lay still.

"No, no, no, Big Boy—you best think twice about dragging your big self on over here!" The man rammed that revolver tight to the girl's temple hard enough that her head bent sideways.

I slowed my pace and held a hand out, no coincidence it was the same one that gripped my cocked Colt. I did not shake. I kept it aimed, straight and true at that man's head. But I was too far and I knew it. Worse, he knew it.

That smug jackass smiled, thumbed back the hammer on his revolver, and a cry of fear escaped from around the kerchief in the girl's mouth. I stopped, but I did not lower my gun.

"All the way, Big Boy. Drop that thing and back away."

I stood still, weighing my paltry options.

Jack moaned. He was alive, thank God.

"Do it now, if you please." Again, Fancy Collar smiled.

I ground another of my back teeth into powder.

I saw that gun he held to the girl's pretty head looked a whole lot like my Schofield. Damn him all to hell.

"Nnn . . . no, no, Roamer! No!" Jack had looked up at me, his head wobbling. Blood, bright and shiny, covered half his face, his usually wild nest of silver hair now matted with the red-black blood.

Without looking down at him, Fancy Collar lashed out with his right boot, kicking Jack hard in the side of the chest. Jack wheezed, collapsing once more.

"Do as I say or the girl and the old man both die."

"And you?" I said, difficult to squeeze out the words from between my gritted teeth. "If they're dead, then you know I'll kill you."

The girl whimpered again.

"Not if I kill you first." Fancy Collar giggled. "And I am an exceedingly excellent shot, in case you are wondering. Besides, I will then have nothing to lose and you will have lost that foul creature." He glanced at Jack, then shook the girl as if rattling a wind chime of bone. "And this lovely creature."

"And if I do?"

"Ah, the negotiator. I did not realize on the train you had such depth to your character, Big Boy. Such, how shall I put it . . . ?"

"Don't bother, you gabby fool," I said. "Answer my question."

"Straight to it, eh? Good for you. If I were to negotiate with you, I would offer this: You toss aside that Colt, then you back away as far as you care to before hightailing it for that hill." He nodded toward the steep slope at the far end of town, the one Jack and I had descended earlier. "I will not cause further harm to either of these . . . unfortunate creatures. But they will be coming with me. Insurance and all that, should you decide to get a wild hair and follow me."

"No," I said, not moving except to shake my head.

"Fine," he said, and jerked the Schofield—yep, definitely my gun—at Jack's head. I saw Fancy Collar's finger on the trigger. It bunched and a sneer spread across his mouth. He was going to do it, going to kill my pard with my own gun.

"No! No—don't do it!" I shouted as loud as I could.

The sneer spread into a smile, but he didn't move his eyes from Jack, nor did he raise the gun.

I tossed the Colt, wondering not for the first time in my life how I managed to land myself and my friend in another boiling stewpot of misfortune.

"Good boy," said Fancy Collar. He swung the Schofield around, leveled it on me, and his sneer widened. "Now, here's where you leave us. For good."

To hell with it, I thought. I've reached my end. And what does it matter? Jack's likely to be addled forever, I failed the girl, and this man is bent on killing everyone in sight.

Then a curious thing happened—the girl shouted. She sounded strong and there was a sharpness to her that appeared from nowhere.

"No!" she growled. "You leave him be! Leave him alone!"

I admit I did not know what to make of this, but her moment of boldness saved my skin.

Fancy Collar did not look at her, but his teeth showed behind tight-pulled lips. He kept the gun on me for a long moment more, as if weighing a decision, then spat a sigh of disgust and let the barrel drop a couple of inches. "You may back up now, Big Boy."

Something odd had happened, but he was still playing with me, like the barn cat who has all but killed the field mouse. The temptation to escape to freedom is a thick root in all living things, has to be. Otherwise, why was I doing what he said? Somehow she had bought me time and I wasn't about to waste it.

"That's it, keep it going. I'll shout when you can stop. You hear that? You answer me . . ." He smiled wide so I could see, and then he jammed the snout of the Schofield into the girl's head again. ". . . or else!"

"I heard you, jackass." I'd meant it to sound bold, big, raw, but my voice was a thin, tired croak. Still, I hoped it would rile him. Though calling him a name might not be the smartest thing I could have done.

He sighed as if he were onstage. "I'll give you marks for that. But only because you amuse me. My name is Henry. Surname of Delacroix—no 'jackass' to be found. I dare say you may have heard of me!"

He was shouting now, wanting to make certain I heard him ramble on about his name. I shook my head and kept stepping backward slowly. I had to figure out how to get Jack and the girl out of there. This man killed all his cohorts, surely he wouldn't put up with Jack's cantankerous ways for any measure of time. If Jack was even going to be among the living much longer.

"I am a Delacroix of Savannah! We are a bold and fearless lot! And you, sir, are apparently not of the same cloth."

"And thank the Lord for it!" I shouted. I couldn't help myself. I can only take so much braggadocio at one time, no matter how dire the situation. But Savannah . . . that would explain his drippy Southern accent.

Truth is, I do think I had heard of his clan somewhere along the line. But not in a favorable light. During the war, I believe, something to do with slaving. Another reason to hate the bastard.

"I will not release my fearful hold on the girl until you are up that hillside, standing like the shaggy-haired goat you are, surveying your meager kingdom. And only then will I make preparation to move onward. Is that clear? Any sign that you are performing a well-intentioned but foolhardy mission of retrieval of your friends here will result in their quick deaths. By bullet. To the head. Need I go on?"

"I heard you . . . Henry. Jackass. Delacroix."

And do you know what? That smug bastard chuckled. In truth, I was thankful for it. When I am angry, I say things that more often than not should have been left unspoken to rattle in this hollow bone-gourd I call a head.

As I passed the oddly propped corpse of the first man we'd seen Delacroix shoot, I looked to see if he wore a gun belt, something I'd not done earlier. It was there, a common black leather affair strapped around his middle, but the holster and bullet loops were empty. Could be Delacroix had stripped him of them before they had emerged on the street. Before he'd berated, then killed the man. I moved on. At least I had my rifle back with Tiny.

I'd get my Schofield back from Delacroix. It had been with me a long time and I vowed to get it back, hopefully before it killed anyone else. I slowed near the body, glancing at Henry Delacroix, and I thought I saw him fidget. I was still in his sight line.

I finally turned my back on the madman and made my slow way up the hillside, switchbacking high enough that he might feel safe in leaving the street.

Jack hadn't done as I'd said and gone to retrieve our mounts. Not that I expected he would. I wouldn't if he'd told me to. He had stuck to his plan and no doubt had hoped I would come to my senses and follow it, too. Well, I hadn't, and now we were all floating in bubbling stew.

I stopped and stared, my arms folded across my chest. I had to know what Delacroix was planning. I'd let go their horses. Did he have other mounts? I suspected not. He likely knew they'd been freed, as he'd shot his pals, and one of them must have given him the bad news. Was he planning on tracking down the horses?

Almost as if by magic, I saw movement to my right, on the outer edge of the tiny town proper. It was the horses, clustered tight and milling around something. One at a time, their heads went down, each one nervous and scouting, it seemed, for some unseen danger. They'd found a feed for themselves. So much for them wanting freedom. They must have sensed me thinking about the dangers of life as a free critter in these parts.

If he found them, he'd be a-horseback once more and I'd have a more difficult time following. I saw the pretty bay acting as if she were the boss of the little band of horses, nudging the others with her nose and head shoves, and hoofing at the ground.

I reckoned Tiny Boy might have found a match in her. Maybe later. I didn't feel in the least bit good about scrambling the rest of the way up the hillside, finding Tiny and Mossy, and what? Retrieving a rifle? At this distance I couldn't hit the man. I am a solid shot, but this was far beyond even a trick-shot carnival man's efforts. Right now I had to keep my eyes on any movement down below in the town, had to see if Delacroix was going to discover those horses.

I didn't have long to wonder or wait. He'd trussed Jack's arms behind his back, then left him flopped where he'd clubbed him at the end of the street. My old chum appeared to move a little here and there on his own. I breathed a cautious sigh and hoped he'd stick with it. He's a hell of a fighter, so that would help.

I tracked Delacroix's progress through the town as much as I was able. He'd disappeared with the girl into a large building at the far end of town, close to the terminus with the once-upon-a-time creek. The structure, a two-story affair, gray boarded and sporting sprung planks here and there like whiskers on a snoring drunk, sat on the northern side of the street. They stayed in there for several minutes. In that time I heard both their voices rise and fall, as if they were arguing. The girl had spunk, I'd give her that. She had a Schofield pressed tight to her head not minutes before, and she still managed to put up a fight.

I heard a couple of loud slamming noises. They tensed me. I deliberated—I could hotfoot it up the hill, get my rifle and cartridges, and make it back in time to . . . do what? If I sneaked back down there, Delacroix might put a bullet in her head and then Jack's, because he could. He didn't seem to care about much of anything, save his own bloated family name.

No, there would be little point in doing that. I'd be better off to bide my time and see what his next move was. At least I had a paltry truce with the killer.

I didn't have long to wait. He emerged alone from the back of the building, paused once he was in the lane, and waved his arms wide over his head as if summoning me. He kept it up, so I stood and did the same, looking like I was a big old bird flexing featherless wings. Hell, I didn't know what else to do. It seemed to appease him.

He scouted for a minute or so, came right upon the damned clot of four horses, and not a one of them made more than a step here and there to get away from him. Tame as puppies.

He held out his hand and they all crowded around. He was probably feeding them lump sugar.

Then he slipped hackamores, at least that's what they looked like from my distance, over the heads of two, the pretty bay being one, and the dapple gray the other. He tied them to a lone withered post sticking up like a skinny thumb, then made a lunge for a third horse. That one skittered away.

He shouted, "You get your ass back here, horse!" That much I heard, plain as my face is homely.

The horse did not comply. He tried the fourth. It did the same as the other and loped out of his reach. Instead of trying to gentle it, he stood his ground, shouted another blurt of anger, then shucked that Schofield. Before I could shout, "No!" he shot that horse, then took aim and did the same to the first that had offended him.

They both were solid shots and each horse dropped to its knees as if poleaxed. They wobbled like that, snorting heavily, their sides heaving, their heads canting left, then right. Dust boiled up from their straining nostrils. The second one fell first and dropped to its side, its barrel heaving, gasping. The first horse he shot did much the same, as if mimicking its pal. Never had I seen such brutality. He didn't even walk to them and deliver a final bullet to ease their passing. Bastard.

I am not a man who dives headfirst into what some call the Good Book—I have my own way of going about worship. Mainly, it's a deep, abiding respect for, and awe of, the natural world. If a god made it, then so be it. I have to trust that he or she or it knows how grateful I am for it, each day of my life. It is enough for me. I do not share my thoughts with anyone else other than Tiny Boy and Maple Jack. That, too, is enough.

But at that moment, seeing that raw knob of a man seething in his own anger, I prayed for something to lay him low right then and there. Nothing heavenly happened.

What did happen was more surprising to me than any appearance of a god would have been. The girl ran out of the back door of that same two-story building, arms still bound, it seemed, behind the back, but no kerchief around her mouth.

She screamed at him, would have slapped him across the face, I am certain of it, had her arms been free. But she bolted right up to him and shouted at his face. I did not hear the words, but the rage in her voice was apparent.

Much to my surprise, he stood there and took it as he had earlier in the street when she'd saved my skin, and did not hit her as I feared he would. Had he fallen for her beauty, too? I did not like to think so, though that would be something in her favor, a strand of hope. Jack would not fare so well against such a rage. Should he even be conscious. The man might decide to kill Jack and be done with him, especially now that he likely had one less horse than he needed.

Still, her outburst was welcome, if unexpected. I had an ally in her. One with fire in her veins. That heartened me.

I also realized that the man was an idiot. He set himself up well, considering he was watched from the hill by me, a blatant adversary, and had killed off his helpers. He had need of at least three horses, if what he threatened was truly his plan, that of taking the girl and Jack along with him as hostages, as insurance, as he said. Now he only had two horses, unless he had another one secreted away somewhere. Not likely.

I waited there a few long moments, knowing the day's light would be gone in an hour or so. Was Delacroix going to make a push on out of there before nightfall? That would be reckless, indeed. Stuck out on the trail in the dark, whatever trail there might be. I wished I had Jack's knowledge of this part of the country.

I had my own, and precious little use that was going to be in trailing them. Still, two horses, one of them overworked carrying double riders, wouldn't travel quickly nor leave too light a trail. I had Tiny Boy and Ol' Mossback to keep me company, both seasoned trail cutters, so I should make decent time. I would not be able to get too close, though, for fear Delacroix might detect me and do something rash.

I didn't have to wait much longer. They had disappeared back toward the tall building at the end of the row, Delacroix leading the horses. The beasts fidgeted and danced more than they had before, which wasn't saying much. But that lack of fire might also work in my favor, keeping them slowed ahead of me. And what of the loot Delacroix and his men had taken from the train safe?

I had pictured it as a heavy haul, sacks of coins, paper money, bonds, what else could the humble-seeming train have been carrying? That, of course, was the golden answer—the little transport was unlikely to attract attention, and so would make an ideal run on which to ferry valuable goods. I hoped he had scored a big, heavy haul and that he was as greedy as I suspected him of being—yet another slowing factor.

To my disappointment, they soon walked into view again, the girl on one horse, Delacroix leading both beasts by the reins. The riderless horse wore what looked to be two laden, oversize saddlebags behind the cantle. They did not shift much, though the animal was only walking, but they looked solid and heavy.

Delacroix halted the beasts before the still-prone Jack and said something, too low for me to hear. Then he toed Jack in the gut with a boot. Jack stirred, rolling over on his side. His head was a dark, bloody mess, but the bleeding looked to have slowed. The patch of earth on which he'd rested his head was darker than the drying blood on his face.

Jack spoke, again too low for me to make out. But it could not have been anything flattering for Delacroix to hear, for the killer lashed out with two quick hard kicks to Jack's sagged belly. Jack convulsed, curled up in a baby's position, and I shouted at the same time the girl did.

She screamed, "Stop it!"

I shouted, "Hey! Damn you!"

I am unsure whose barked words had the most effect on the bastard, but he spun, looked from the girl to the hillside, toward me, and I thought I saw his shoulders drop. It was a theatrical motion, as if he felt a momentary twinge of defeat. But he recovered, and turned his attentions back to his victim. If only to show me and the girl, no doubt, who held the reins. He gave Jack another kick. Then he shouted, "Now get up, old man! On your feet!"

Jack panted a moment, and tried to drag a knee forward and under himself, but with his hands lashed tight around his back, his head swimming, and now a kicked gut, there was little he could do.

Delacroix swore, loud enough for me to hear, shifted the bunched reins to his left hand, and grabbed the collar of Jack's

buckskin tunic. He'd taken off his fur-lined coat earlier in the day when the sun pinned itself high in the blue sky and warmed us from above. Now he would be cold all night, and ailing. And there I was, staring down at the scene from on high like a dunderhead.

With Jack's feeble efforts, the killer managed to drag him to his feet, and steered the staggering mountain man to the horse with the already heavy burden of what I assumed was the thieves' takings from the train. He untied Jack's hands and re-tied them in front of him.

Jack was unable to climb into the saddle. He kept weaving and staggering. I would like to say it was all for show, that he had a plan of some sort. But Jack was in a bad way.

Finally the foul killer leaned Jack face-first against the left side of the horse, walked to the right side, and through sheer willpower, as Jack is not a light man, dragged poor Jack up onto that saddle.

He at least tried one more time to get Jack seated in the saddle, but my old friend could not seem to make his legs do his bidding and fork the saddle. Delacroix did what I'd hoped he would not, he left Jack facedown over the saddle, and lashed his wrists with a rope, which he ran under the horse's belly, then looped and cinched it tight around Jack's ankles. As if he were tying on a dead man.

Riding like that is no way to cure a head wound. I know, hav-ing been in a similar position once, several years back, when I'd found myself ambushed by a bounty man and his assistant, a crass woman named Pretty Polly, who was anything but fetch-ing. They mistook me for a wanted man, not the first time that's happened, and had managed to subdue me and lash me draped across Tiny Boy, in a similar fashion as Jack now found himself in.

The girl spoke sharp words to him again, and he raised a

long finger, pointing it at her in warning. She held her tongue. He mounted up behind her, seated too damn close for my liking, and with a lead rope from Jack's mount to a saddle ring on the horse he rode; Henry Delacroix and Annette, the pretty girl in blue, began their walk on out of town, leading my half-dead best friend and two sacks of stolen goods.

I was about to turn and bolt up the hillside. I didn't want to waste any time in retrieving our mounts and gear and heading back down after them. Delacroix once more surprised me. He angled his horse back around to face me, stopped, and shouted.

"Hey, you! Big Boy!" His voice carried well on the still valley air.

I stared a moment, then waved one arm wide to indicate I heard him.

"You try to follow us and I will kill the old man and the girl. Of course, if you feel you want to risk their lives to get at me, by all means, have at it. I shall be waiting. Elsewise, leave off and no one gets harmed. The girl will be taken to civilization and, well, let's say her fate is of no concern to you. As for the old man, I will turn him loose, alive, somewhere on the trail. Unless he continues to give me difficulties, that is!" His forced cackle taunted me.

"You leave him here!" I had to try. "No reason for you to take the old man!"

I could almost hear Maple Jack growling at this poor assessment of his age.

"Oh, I'd be happy to leave him here. Dead, that is! Now you shut up and back the hell off, otherwise he's done for. The girl, too!"

"Okay, okay! But if you harm ether one of them, so help me, Delacroix, I will—"

He interrupted me: "What, Big Boy? What is it you are going to do to me? Huh?" He cackled again, sounding like a man two steps away from doing something bad. I said nothing.

A few moments passed. I saw no quick movements, heard no gunshots or screams or groans. I took that as a promising sign.

"Okay then," he shouted. "We will now take our leave. But heed me, Big Boy. I will not be trifled with. Adios!"

The last of the man's warning echoed its way up the canyon before peeling apart like dry bark in a breeze. I heard every word.

I only hoped Jack would keep his temper in check.

CHAPTER TWENTY-ONE

With the need for immediate caution now gone, I stomped my way up the slope. I reached the spot where we'd tied Tiny and Mossy. They were both still there, though Mossy had lain down, shifting his load of Jack's gear. I nudged him to his feet and straightened the load, biting back the urge to shout out of anger and frustration. All this was my fault, sure as the day was dwindling, and I did not know how to make it right. The only thing I had to do, could do, was keep on their trail. At a distance. And wait for an opportunity to present itself—or make one.

"Come on," I said, tugging Tiny's reins. He seemed to sense my mood and didn't bother with the usual nips and belligerent head tosses he offers when he's hungry and surly. In that, we are very much alike. I still marvel, though I should not by now, at his intuitive ways. Mossy's lead line was lashed to Tiny Boy's saddle and he followed along, uncomplaining as ever.

I reached the spot where I'd stood for far too long watching the proceedings down below. There they were, two dark shapes moving westward. In minutes they'd disappear into a steep canyon that looked to be an old road, perhaps the primary route, leading in and out of Sapphire City.

I rummaged in one of Jack's saddlebags and pulled out his prize brass collapsible spyglass. I tugged it open, the warm clicks reminding me of Jack as the piece slid into full length. I twisted the rings, and managed to focus in on my quarry.

Jack looked like hell, his head and his feet bouncing with

each slow step taken by the overburdened horse. His mass of silver hair, what wasn't matted to his head with dried blood, waved and bobbed like a dirty cloud.

"Hang in there, Jack. I'm coming. I am coming . . ."

Delacroix had one arm around the girl's midsection, and was talking to her, his cheek and chin pressed close to her neck. She looked to be wincing. Perhaps she was whip-smart by then, had experienced his raging ways, and knew she had to put up with his attentions, unwanted though they surely were.

I watched the two horses wind their way, in no great hurry, out of town, headed west toward Hells Canyon and the Seven Devils range, if I remembered correctly. What lay before that? A whole lot of terrain. Was it decent? Forgiving? It had been years since I'd been out that way. I had to reach them soon. The longer they rode, the worse Jack would get. And the girl, she had to be far beyond the horizon of happy and healthy. What had Delacroix subjected her to since thieving her from the train? I did not dwell on the foul visions flaring in my mind.

Before they entered the narrow canyon that would take them from my view, Delacroix turned his head and looked right at me. I swear, he looked right into the fat end of that spyglass. And the bastard smiled. Then they disappeared from sight between the narrow rock walls.

I collapsed the spyglass in on itself, stuffed it back into the saddlebag, tied it closed, and mounted up on Tiny Boy. I knew where I was headed, I knew who I was headed for, and I knew what I needed to do, but I didn't know when or how I could do it. That is much of life, I reckon.

We switchbacked our way down the slope. At the far end of town I stopped to retrieve Jack's old cap-and-ball war cannon from where it had been left in the dirt. I brushed off the dust and snugged it deep inside one of his saddlebags, certain he'd get the chance to wear it once more.

Close by lay the bodies of Delacroix's men. He had taken their lives and their guns, too; that much was plain. I did not inspect further.

Though Hector and Ginger Whiskers had been in league with that vicious killer, I could not suppress a twinge, however slight, of pity for the two, as well as for the dead man at the other end of the street. But that was all I was willing to offer. Nothing more.

"Let's go," I said again, mounting up. We rode away from the ghostly wreck that was Sapphire City, leaving its resident mountain spirit with a whole lot more to be angry about.

CHAPTER TWENTY-TWO

It's odd to track a man who knows you're trailing him, who expects you to tag along, but also knows he's holding the cards that count. I didn't have a thing. I was betting on a hunch, on hope, on him slipping up or overlooking something. And so it went that first night. He had two horses, both tired, plus three people, himself included, who all had to be bone-tired.

I didn't like to admit it, but I still wasn't right following my kerfuffle with the wolverine, the snowslide, the elements, the train and everything that happened there. I was better than I had been, because of Jack's help. But if I stood any chance of dealing Delacroix a crippling blow, I needed sleep. Trouble was, I had to keep alert lest I stumble on the man in the dark.

For all I knew, he was ten paces ahead of me, encamped and waiting. Or he was fool enough to ride all night. He might be fool enough, but I didn't think those horses would make it much beyond a couple of hours after they departed Sapphire City.

I tracked them with no real effort until daylight was gone. Twice in the waning light I saw them far ahead. If I saw them, he saw me. I kept distance between us. He followed a westerly trail, more a path cut through rabbitbrush than an old road. I thought of the abandoned town. This had to be the primary route in and out. The direction we'd come, over the mountains and through that high pass, was not a trail anyone with sense would travel.

The terrain changed along the flanks of the mountains. I sensed we were coming to water long before I could see it. The land sloped to a broad flat before the next spine of peaks. Before me, in the middle, brown grasses tufted in hummocks as they do in areas of wet. Jack calls them ankle snappers because they're so treacherous to walk or ride through. I always thought of them as big grassy heads poking up out of the earth, as if they were underground dwellers curious to see what this place had to offer. They always seem paused, as if undecided about shouldering their way out of their earthy homes.

I should not have indulged in such fanciful thinking, but should have filled my mind with strategies and cunning plans. Poor Jack will have to hang in there and wait for me to figure out when and where I can barge in on Delacroix and lay him low.

This is not how Dumas would devise a hero's plans, but that is why I am no scribe. I am a traveler in life, a man in quest of something, peace, perhaps, that after all these years I am beginning to suspect does not exist. But that will not stop me from searching.

By the time all that blather had churned through my shaggy head, we made it to the water source, a seasonal stream as wide as a wagon is long, with rivulets here and there burbling around rocks of varying sizes, most fist-size. It had been a welcome wet latter half of the summer, and the rains had continued on into autumn, accounting for the decent flow. Delacroix had crossed here.

I hopped down off Tiny Boy, loosened his cinch, did the same with Mossy, and let them drink their fill. I also drank, then filled our water skins and canteens, taking care to ensure the bungs were well seated and thonged tight. I wanted no surprises ahead, and a lack of water for me or my four-legged chums would offer unwanted challenges.

I knelt and studied the tracks, noting many clustered along the water's edge. A man's boots—had to be those of Delacroix, as Jack wore thick-soled moccasins—sunk in enough here and there to tell me some version of what had taken place. I traced a drag trail a few feet to the left, southward along the low, rock-pocked bank, and made out a depression where something thick had settled. Jack? Could be Delacroix dragged my pard off the horse to give the beast a rest.

I am adequate at reading sign, though the markings left here required no great skill. I learned much of what I know from Maple Jack, and more from an exiled Navajo I helped out of a scrape in a dingy little town in Utah several years ago.

I know not what happened to him after we parted. He was a good man, though he carried great grief that hung on him like a heavy yoke. I suspect that unseen burden would eventually crush him. Time hastens this if a man cannot find a way to help old wounds to close. Pick at them and they never heal, only fester and bubble and spread.

I scanned the horizon. Delacroix had to know the pickle he'd put himself in by shooting his spare horses. If he lost another one now, he'd kill Jack and ride the last horse to death with himself, the girl, and his train loot. And then, to ease the horse's burden, he'd kill the girl and keep the loot. Men like Delacroix care for one thing—themselves—and keeping that safe is all they care for.

I saw no bodies flopped in the brittle grasses that reached halfway to my knees. I kept searching, enjoying the chance to stretch my legs, my back, my shoulders, and to ease Tiny's load. I'd prefer to walk along with him, my choice when I had the leisure to do so, which was most of the time. But today I needed to keep as close as I dared to the killer and his charges.

At that, I reckoned I was a mile or more behind them. Plenty of distance should he come snooping in the night for a chance to lay me low. But not so far that should I decide to do the same to him, I couldn't make it in quick time. Only problem with that was I had no plan that wouldn't put the girl or Jack in a hard spot.

Delacroix was taking no pains to disguise his trail—why would he? And the notion that he was toying with me, that he would kill me from a distance, was topmost in my mind. I suppose I would do that were I him, a creature pursued by someone who'd witnessed him murder beasts and men. And besides, he'd told me his name. Unless it was a lie to put me off his scent, not likely, then any reason he had for allowing me to live had evaporated when he'd uttered his name to me.

I let those worries flutter off on a fresh quiver of breeze while I tightened cinches and mounted back up. Tiny grunted and Mossy lowered his head and fell in line, uncomplaining as always, and as unlike Maple Jack as I was like Tiny Boy.

By the time twilight succumbed to full dark, I was ready to either fall off Tiny's ample back or keep going, head nodding and bobbing, angry with myself for not being more concerned about my friend's life and that of the girl. Tiny guided us up a rise and I saw the winking orange flicker of a flame, though far enough off that it was little more than a match flare in the dark.

As if cued, Tiny's ears perked forward. We both flexed our nostrils and detected the faint tang of woodsmoke carried our way on a light breeze. With luck, Jack and the girl would be able to grab needed rest. And with further luck, Delacroix was as wrung out as I was and would sit in a dozing daze by his little fire. I suspected that would be the case, but I would take precautions.

I backed my little train on down the slope where we could camp without our own humble fire being seen. It didn't take long to unburden, then tether Ol' Mossback and Tiny Boy. They were both trail-sore and tired. Jack had had the forethought to gather a couple of armloads of dry wood at our last campsite, and in little time I had a small fire snapping, decent enough to cook on.

The night was chilly but not painful. I would not need to feed the devouring fire-beast all night merely to keep warm. The more wood I could save for future fires, the better. I would rekindle the fire for coffee come morning. A few hours of sleep, with a rifle across my lap and my sheath knife at hand, would make that early cup of coffee all the finer.

As soon as the fire could stand on its own, I watered the boys, then doled out a lashing of oats. Mossy looked about ready to doze off in his nose bag. I rubbed between his ears, then on down his forehead, in part to keep him awake so he'd finish his meal and in part because I wanted him to know our unfortunate situation would take a turn for the better, hopefully come tomorrow.

I broke out a meager poke of vittles—a length of elk jerky, amply peppered, as Jack is wont to prepare it—and two rocklike knobs of hardtack. They aren't long on flavor, offer even less in the way of moisture, but they tend to expand once in the gut. They fill a man well enough.

The trick with Jack's trail rocks, or gut busters, as I call them—he growls and curses me when I say that, but grins when he thinks I'm not looking—is getting the cursed knobs into swallowable condition. A man has to have a decent set of choppers to grind them into something manageable, but I'm set on that score. I do my best to take care of my teeth.

I've seen enough men with blackened teeth and swollen jaws and agonized looks on their faces. I've heard plenty of howls and shrieks and low groans of pain from men straddled by a blood-covered fellow with a set of smithy's tongs jammed deep in their mouths.

I pick my teeth after each meal with a sliver off a stick, then I rinse with water and spit it out. A couple of years ago, I bought a tiny brush made in England with boar bristles that I use daily to keep my teeth clean. Jack scoffs at this, calling it foofaraw, but I still have all my teeth and he has had to yank three of his. I also nibble on fragrant herbs when I get the chance.

Must have been the belly full of gut busters, but I slept like a rock. Then a sound woke me. I didn't know what it was, but I snapped my eyes wide open, and didn't move other than that. It was still dark, though as I looked up, I saw the sky purpling from behind me. I'd been facing westward when I sat down hours before.

I hadn't moved much at all in my sleep, a sure sign I'd been dog-tired. My rifle was laid across my lap, my hand ready to slip down two inches and grasp the hilt of my sheath knife. Of course, none of that meant a thing considering I was alone, and left myself wide open to be shot by Delacroix.

I'd only intended to catnap through the night. On the trail I tend to be a jittery, cautious sleeper, used to being alone. But I have been known to doze off deep and hard. Often, Tiny Boy will alert me with a snort or throaty nicker. I glanced over at him and Mossy, and both were still where I'd picketed them. Tiny swung his head toward me, but Mossy was still asleep.

There was that sound again, and now I knew it for what it was—Mossy snoring. More like a grating, wheeze. Not nearly as rough as Jack's rumbles. All appeared normal, so I gained my feet. I kept the rifle in one hand and stretched tall and wide, turning slowly and working my shoulders up and down. Sleeping leaned against a rock, even one padded with a saddle blanket, is not any more pleasant than it sounds.

I woke later than I intended. I'd wanted to grab a few hours of sleep, three at the most, then get back on the trail. Still, I hankered for a cup of hot coffee. Or maybe three or four such cups. It would be an indulgence, but I knew from past experience it would set me up for the day.

Before I stoked what coals I hoped remained of my previous night's fire, I climbed back up the rise and scouted. I saw no speck of distant flame from a campfire. Must be they were still asleep. I took that as a sign and ambled back down the slope. While the fire snapped and popped and began working its magic on the coffee pot, I packed up the rest of camp. It didn't take long as I hadn't unloaded much, only what I'd needed.

By the time the coffee bubbled and rose on a feather of steam to twitch my nose with its bitter, heady scent, the sky was bright enough for me to see long distances. I climbed the rise once more and saw no fire, no telling bumps on the landscape. I squinted, scanning the flat, and saw nothing resembling two horses and three people traveling away from me. I sighed and stomped back down the slope to retrieve Jack's spyglass, though I knew it would be a fruitless search. I had underestimated Delacroix. He was on the trail, chuckling to himself, and for good reason. He'd tricked me.

But I had the upper hand—I was rested, and of more importance, so were my steeds. My animals were in better flesh than his and we weren't slowed by two begrudging travelers. The spyglass, as I suspected, showed nothing more than the wide, rolling valley before me.

I drank down as much coffee as I could. I managed to scorch my lips and blaze a fiery trail down my throat with the hot, black liquid, but I'd be hanged before I waste it. I cooled off the pot with water, which I then caught in the fry pan and dumped back into a waterskin. I'd only made enough coffee for three cups, and somehow managed to mount up with the last cupful in one hand. I sipped it as we picked our way north for several hundred yards, then we angled west to cut their trail.

It didn't take long to reach their campsite. I climbed down and held my palm over the embers of their fire. It was cold.

Then a thought came to me—what if that fire had been a ruse and they'd trekked west through the night? I had underestimated Delacroix thus far. Who's to say I hadn't again?

If not, they had grabbed a few hours of rest, then had a cold breakfast. I nosed around the site and found what I suspect was Jack's resting spot. Soft, rounded heel marks, probably from his moccasins, were dug into the sandy earth. Nearby I spied two round divots, might be from his knees. I saw no hand prints, so it was possible Delacroix had tied Jack's hands behind him once more for the night.

If I read the sign right, it looked as though Jack had struggled to get up on his own, rocking off his feet and onto his knees. Which told me he might be feeling less addled today, perhaps even able to sit a saddle on his own.

There was sign of the girl as well. Her boot heels were smaller, close by those of Delacroix. I took in as much as I could, and found a few finger marks in the soft ground that might have been made by the girl. They seemed small, more slender than those of a man. Was she tied?

I didn't know how far ahead of me they were, but standing there trying to decipher whatever sign they left behind at the meager campsite was fast becoming a waste of time. I mounted up and followed. As with the previous day, Delacroix had taken no pains to disguise their back trail. I assumed that meant he would try to kill me at some point.

Early gray light was elbowed out of the way by a bright, sunny morning, and the bold disk of sun rose higher, warming me and the boys.

The sun was not yet overhead when the promise of clear sky gave way to a slow-moving bulk of gray that began eating up the pretty blue. I felt it before I saw it, that seeping cold that crawls into even the tightest-buttoned coats and tugged-up collars.

Before I squinted at the horizon above the peaks ahead, I

knew I was going to see it, that mass creeping up on me from the west. I've been in the open long enough to know the signs, and in October, and fresh off an early-season blizzard, I was gun-shy. This was shaping up to be another ragged hunk of foul weather.

Still on their trail, we'd been kicking along at a steady pace, but I was worried as I'd not caught sight of them in the distance. I took cold comfort in the fact that the terrain had sprouted more hills and deeper gullies between.

From somewhere ahead, I heard a series of cracking sounds, as if I were hearing shifting river ice from a distance, but no, too early in the season. Then I knew—gunshots. I reined up, cocked an ear, and did my best to pick out more. I was not disappointed. The sounds of at least another five shots reached me. A gunfight? Did Delacroix run into somebody? The law? I doubted it would be anyone the railroad had hired; they wouldn't know where to look. Then who?

I wasted no more time listening. Whatever was happening wasn't good. But it was farther away than I anticipated. We ate up rises and thundered down gulleys, one after another, making steady progress toward the next range of mountains. But still I caught no sight of them, nor did I hear more shots. The wind bore down on us from the west, carrying its own sound and making distance difficult to measure. It looked as though my daylong suspicion that Delacroix had taken little rest was becoming a certainty.

CHAPTER TWENTY-THREE

I crested a wide rise and the vista opened before me, giving way to a broad valley floor. The expanse at the base of the slope was almost a dry moat to cross before the next range, a mass of snow-crusted rock and shadow. It rose from the land before me, jutting high and proud, running south to north and scarred with vertical fissures like wrinkles in a man's coat sleeve.

All this I saw in a matter of seconds after topping the rise, but it was the scene below me, at the base, that froze my breath—one of the most gruesome scenes I have ever had the ill luck to witness. I counted five horses splayed on the crusted brown earth, boulders littering the scene, two of the horses draped in bizarre poses over these rocks. Two others, perhaps more, were not dead, but twitched and trembled. I counted two saddles as my eye roved the scene.

Take it in, I told myself, breathe deeply and take it in, discover all you can about what Delacroix must surely have done. The gunshots on the wind, this was the reason. And then my eyes stopped, skittered back to what they surely could not have seen. A man, half-pinned beneath one of the horses. He was not moving, unlike the horse laid across his legs, which thrashed more than the others that seemed alive.

What could this mean? I searched the scene below, spotted four horses with three riders in the distance, too far away to catch, though I knew who they were. I resisted the temptation to tug out the spyglass. It must be Delacroix and, I hoped, Jack and the girl, too. To my immense relief the three figures were all seemingly upright. Then another thought doused that spark of hope—what if I was wrong and it was Jack down below?

I ranged my eyes back to the scene. Danger of being shot seemed slim, so I urged Tiny and Mossy down the slope, as fast as I dared, switchbacking down the same scuffed trail Delacroix had likely taken. I glanced skyward once more—that bleak cloud mass had boiled closer. I suppressed a groan.

By the time I made it to the bottom and tied Tiny and Mossy a dozen yards away—the sight and smell of more dead horses did nothing to keep either of them calm—another of the beasts succumbed to death with a final gasp and tremble. But a new sound replaced its last wheezes. This one was from a man.

"Hellll . . ."

He was either swearing at his own pain or trying to ask for help. Once I found him I'd figure it out. It didn't take long, but I had to keep saying, "Hey, fella? Where are you? Keep talking, I can't find you."

He did his best to keep up his end of the conversation, but once I found him, backed into a dark wedge of space beneath the angle of a boulder, I saw why I hadn't spied him from above. He was all but hidden. He'd kicked and scuffed the earth before the gap with his boots, maybe when he'd crawled on in there.

"You can come on out of there," I said, leaning down with caution, the business end of my rifle aimed at him.

He didn't answer, but looked to be struggling to keep his eyes open. Drops of sweat stippled his face.

"You hurt?" A dumb question on my part, given his situation, but I wanted to know if he was a danger, the lure in a trap. I kept my ears perked for someone creeping up on me.

He offered the barest nod of his head, but couldn't raise it from the ground. Something glistened on his chin. Spittle? I leaned closer. Blood.

He looked pretty bad. Another amazing insight, Roamer. I leaned closer and noticed his hands both gripped at his belly. "You been shot?" I said, softer, knowing the answer.

Again, he nodded.

"Want me to get you out of there?"

His eyes widened then and his bottommost leg kicked softly, his boot heel jammed into the ground. He gasped, holding it. I thought maybe he was trying to wedge himself even deeper into the crevice.

"I'm not going to harm you, fella. I'll help you if I can. But you have to trust me, okay?"

He stared, swallowed, and opened his mouth. Blood oozed out.

I set down my rifle and held up my hands.

"Okay," he said in a whisper, then closed his eyes again.

Moving him was likely one of the worst things I could do for him, but if he was gutshot, which it looked like to me, he was a dead man anyway. Might be he could tell me something useful before he expired. I'd do my best to make him comfortable in the time he had left. Judging from the quick, ragged breaths coming from his blood-bubbled mouth, he was within spitting distance of the end already.

Much like tugging free a stuck-on plaster, there was only one way to go about this. As gently as I could, I grabbed his lower shoulder, laid a hand atop his leg, and after a quick, private thought of "One, Two, Three!" I eased him out of there.

The movement dragged a sharp, girlish scream from him, then he either passed out or died, I didn't know which. I winced and looked down at him. I'm a big fellow, and he was not, but he was burlier than I'd first supposed. A smallish-height man, but swarthy, solidly built.

I heard him breathe. I let him catch up. "I'm going to guess you were attacked by a man named Delacroix."

"How'd you . . . ?"

"I am tracking him. He's a killer, a thief, and a kidnapper. But I don't expect any of that will shock you." I was trying to keep him conscious until I could figure out a next move. Subtle I am not. His eyes were glazing.

I leaned in once more. "Delacroix?"

That did the trick, for I saw a spark of something alight his eyes and he nodded. "Hired me and Cletus . . . Cletus?"

He said the name louder. I glanced twenty feet to my right, saw the top half of the man pinned beneath the now-dead horse.

The swarthy man looked at me. "Cletus?"

I shook my head slowly. He understood. "He your friend?"

"Brother," he said. "My . . . brother."

It was a painful thing to hear. "Sorry," I said. I paused a moment, let him stutter his breaths out and in, then said, "Delacroix hired you?"

"To bring horses." He swallowed. "Supposed to meet him up at . . . Sapphire City . . . said he'd struck it rich, needed horses to haul out the gems . . . said we'd be his partners."

"But you were late getting there?" I said.

He nodded. "Lost our way," he said.

He was still with me. I kept prodding. "He have others with him? A woman? Another man?"

"Yeah . . . pretty girl. Old fella, mad looking . . ." His eyes closed and his breathing softened. I thought he'd died, but in a whisper he said, "Water . . ." He opened his eyes. "So thirsty . . ."

I nodded and ran to Tiny, grabbing my canteen. Before I made it back to the man, his hands had loosened their grip on his gut. His efforts hadn't done any good. His innards spilled out of a belly that had been peppered close-up, the bullets likely drilled right through him. Blood seeped from him.

"Hell," I said, my big useless hands hanging at my sides. I

bent down and closed his eyelids.

I stood and scanned the bloody scene around me. By then the last of the struggling horses was dead. That's when I saw one I recognized. It was the pretty bay mare. She'd made it further than I thought she might, only to die here by that bastard's foul hand.

"Damn you, Henry Delacroix." I stared in the direction I'd seen them ride, topped by a darkening storm-cloud sky. I'd tail them as fast as I was able, but first I had something to do.

Nothing about death is pretty, and I stood in the midst of too much of it, five horses and two men, all bled out. The horses had let loose their last meals, and the steam and stink of blood and muck and fear and desperation—don't tell me those last two don't have their own awful smell—surrounded me.

I retrieved a rope from Mossy, who'd adopted his head-down stance, but still wary, as if one more bad thing might set him off and running, tether or no. I couldn't blame him.

I looped the rope around one of the dead horse's legs and with a couple of heaves was able to raise its legs skyward where it caught, wobbling undecided, before it flopped down onto its other side. That left Cletus, the brother, exposed. His lower half had been crushed by the horse when it had fallen on him. I also saw puckered, burnt bullet holes in his coat.

I bent low and grabbed his wrists. One of his hands still wore a glove, the other was gone, somewhere in all this mess. I dragged him over to his brother, the smaller man whose name I did not know. I laid them out side by side, hands atop one another's, and with a hard throat and teeth tight, I rummaged in their pockets to find identification. I found something in the smaller man's breast pocket.

In tiny, neat script was a ledger book and journal of sorts. Between figures for horses sold and sacks of feed bought, he had recorded the day's weather. "Cloudy, might be rain."

"Sunny, no rain again." Inside the front cover he'd written his name, "Christoph. McSwain, prop. McSwain bros. livery, Dixonville, Washington Territory."

I'd let someone know. I closed the little book, slipped it inside my shirt, and set to the task I had in mind as quickly as I knew how. I draped their hats, which I'd managed to find close by each man's spot of dying, and laid them atop their upturned faces.

"I'm sorry boys. I doubt you were crooked. You got hoodwinked by the devil Delacroix. I'll see to him for you. And I will let your kin or friends know of your whereabouts."

Despite knowing I was losing my prey, losing daylight, losing Jack, I had to cover the brothers from the varmints that would come in the night to feast on this mass of dead flesh. Brothers are a special thing, even when they aren't close. I had one of my own, although he is unaware of our kinship. But that is another story for another time.

Luck was with me and I was able to shift enough rocks to cover the two men, hoping the dead horses would keep the wolves and other curious beasts from unearthing them.

I finished, nodded my head, and said, "Be at peace, boys." It was all I could think of to say. I mounted up, and swigged from the canteen as I dug my boot heels into Tiny Boy's barrel. He didn't take much urging. I sensed he'd had enough of that place, and judging from the slack in the lead line, Ol' Mossy did, too.

We rode westward at a hard clip, faster, I hope, than Delacroix was traveling. I had to catch up with him. And this time I would not keep my distance. A plan was coming together in my mind.

CHAPTER TWENTY-FOUR

I'd seen various piles of gear and supplies in the carnage, most of it flecked with blood, from horse and man. I don't think I would have been tempted to rummage through it even if Jack hadn't gone to his usual solid efforts of packing supplies and food enough to ward off starvation on the trail. But it did tell me that Delacroix had counted on the two brothers not only for horses but also for gear and food. While I hoped he fed the girl and Jack enough to keep them well, I also hoped that bastard was suffering the ill effects of paltry meals, long hours in the saddle, and the gnawing fear only a man pursued can know.

It was enough to hearten me as we galloped forward into the stormy horizon. I hadn't slowed my pace, knowing I'd lost more than an hour tending to the brothers. Raw weather didn't bother me. I'd traveled in it before, on foot and a-horseback, but never was I as driven.

We pounded toward the great jags of mountain, following the killer's trail easily once the snow began. The dusting was a boon for tracking, but such luck wasn't mine for long. The powdery haze soon thickened, until keeping in sight the mountains ahead of me became a trick. Then the wind kicked up.

The truth is, the stiff gusts, whipping across my face with no set schedule, helped clear my view. And that's what got me closer to that bastard than I'd been since Sapphire City. In one sudden sweep of wind, I reined up, shocked to see I'd almost overtaken Delacroix and his captives.

I was close enough that I made out Jack's brown, hunched form sitting the saddle sloppier than he'd ever ridden. The man is capable of a whole lot of things, and one of them is forking a horse. So for him to ride like that, with his head down, meant he was sore, or tied tight, or both.

His left foot had fallen out of the stirrup and he jerked it in circles, trying to find purchase once more with his toes. The knobby terrain and the speed they were traveling hindered his efforts. I imagined his voice, railing and cursing and biting off venom-filled bursts. And then he'd remember he was in the presence of a lady and he'd quiet himself to low growls and menacing grumbles.

The idea of him being too addled to do much for himself, to the point that Delacroix had to lash him to his saddle, was too foul to bear. I chose the first notion and drummed my heels once more into Tiny's ribs.

It looked to me as though Delacroix was headed straight for the taller jags of stone, flanked at their base by dense stands of spruce that dissipated as the peaks clawed skyward. The killer must know of a pass through that foreboding ridge. If he did, it was well hidden, because I could see much of that big jut of rocky mountainside, and while I did spy plenty of clefts that might hide a pass, I doubted one was there.

But there had to be, otherwise why would he let me track him straight in there, backing him up to a wall? Maybe he was riled enough by my presence that he wanted to make a stand. Part of me liked the notion I had rattled him so badly. The other possibility was frightening to think about—Jack and the girl were with him and would suffer his wrath first. A man like Delacroix could only feed his rage for so long by shooting livery-men and horses.

I was not gaining on them so much as they were slowing, but it didn't appear I'd be able to reach them before they disappeared into whatever cavern or chasm or hidey-hole Delacroix must know of. It was going to be a race against daylight, snowfall, wind, a fast-dropping temperature, stamina, and terrain. The closer we raced to the flank of the mountain, the more I had expected to feel some reprieve from the wind, at least, guessing that the lee of the rock-sided giant might offer a lessening of the storm. Instead, it looked to be kicking up more of a fuss.

I glanced northward, to my right, and saw why—a cone of wind-driven snow a mile long, but laid on its side like a long wave on a beach, tumbled and whipped along the base of the range.

Given that I'd felt a driving wind at my back for the past twenty minutes I guessed the two air currents—ramming down the slope face of the mountains and the one behind me—were slamming together, creating even more of the stormy mess we were now galloping into.

That's when I lost sight of them. I wasn't worried. Once I emerged from the funnel of snow and wind, I would locate them again. I'd marked what I was certain was Delacroix's destination, a dark spire of rock flanking a vertical chasm, a cleft that looked as likely as any spot for him to head to.

We reached a generous stand of trees. It took me a few moments to locate the tracks, and when I did, they were already filling in with the wind-driven snow. Northward into the trees, their trail was more visible. I also saw pink splotches now and again alongside the snow-punched tracks. Blood. Had Delacroix sustained a wound in the scuffle with the two brothers? Maybe Jack's head wound had opened again. A new wound doled out by his demonic captor?

The wind played haunting notes as it rushed through the trees. Snow devils whipped about, teasing us. Tiny and Mossy were flagging, their steps becoming more plodding as the snow thickened and the cold increased. I had climbed out of the saddle long before. No sense to burden Tiny with my weight.

My face numbed once more. My hands, claws wrapped in gloves, balled around the reins and held close to my battered wool mackinaw. The top of my head was plenty warm, as I was wearing Jack's fur topper, but this one was his autumn cap and as such he'd not seen the need to sew on earflaps. I could only curse the man so much for this error, as I was no doubt warmer than he was at that moment.

Too early, the dark of night dropped on us, aided by the purple gloom of the storm. The snow, which by then was nearly halfway up my boots, made the trudging slow and tedious. I felt the rocks slide beneath my feet as I jammed them with each step into the still-loose scree, tugging Tiny Boy as I led him along, leaning into the steep hillside. Ol' Mossback followed, head down and resigned to whatever new situation he might find himself in.

I had to be close, and I moved slower with each stride, pausing often and listening, sniffing for woodsmoke, anything. I wish I had half the nose for detection Tiny has, but I am a man and stuck with the sniffer I was born with.

I stopped and tied Tiny's reins tight to the trunk of a stout aspen. I'd go ahead on foot. They had to be close. Or I'd discover the secret passage this man seemed to think existed somewhere in this wall of rock.

Jack claims he has the sniffing abilities of a wolf and can smell the stink off a beaver den a mile off. I tell him it's his breath backing up in his face, and he howls and whips up a cloud of frothy rage and stomps off. Works every time.

As if on cue, I heard Jack's voice, close, though with the wind carrying down at me from every which way, it might well be a hundred yards off.

"Ain't nowhere else you can go, boy, leastwise not on a night such as this. I—"

I thought for a flash of a moment that Jack was talking to me. Then Delacroix cut in, screaming. I do not jest, the man was screaming. "Shut up, old man! How do you know, anyway?"

"How do I know? Why you foul whelp! I know because I have roved all over this here mountain range!"

It was indeed Jack I was hearing, lecturing his captor. Tiny nickered low. I hoped the wind carried his sound on downslope. I also hoped Mossy didn't recognize his master's voice and kick up a ruckus. There's little more telltale or annoying than a mule in full throat, and Mossy is quite a singer when he gets rolling.

Jack's voice bubbled out, fast and full, all vigor, no hesitation, as if he'd grown weary of being smacked down like an unwanted child over and over again. "Why, I know every crevice and cranny and I'm telling you this pass you think is here ain't here. You think because that last knob of hills way back had a pass that this one must, too?"

A third voice, softer, but with a sharp edge, cut in. I couldn't make out all the words, but it had to be the girl. "Henry! Enough of this—this man knows better than we do. Trust in him!"

His name came out sharp, as if she were trying to snap him to attention. Then I recalled the way she seemed to have torn into him back in Sapphire City. She was a bold one. Must be he'd fallen so deeply for her, he was willing to let her talk back to him. I had to admit she had sass.

"They said they came this way!" Delacroix had backed off the boil, but he was still testy, with an edge of scolded schoolboy to his voice. "Had to have come this way. I know how to track, I tell you!"

Jack didn't respond, so I did.

"You mean those two men you shot back across the valley? The ones you promised to make partners?"

A pause, then: "They were nothing!" Delacroix said it as if he'd been expecting me. Hell, maybe he thought it was Jack he was still talking with. Maybe he was well and gone in the head.

I decided to prod my luck. "They were brothers," I shouted.

Another pause. I heard something click, ratchet back—the unmistakable throaty sound of a Schofield, my damn gun, being cocked.

"You! You dare encroach?"

I bent low. He didn't know where I was. For once in a long while, the wind was with me. I eased back the hammer on my rifle, hoping the gusting wind might mask the thick-metal clicks. "I dare!" I barked.

I'll give Delacroix this, that devil is quick. He squeezed off a shot at me. Or where he thought I'd be. That poorly placed effort told me plenty. I angled up to my left, taking advantage of another whipping squall that masked me. It also masked a jag of granite that waged a sudden war with my game knee. I tamped a groan and kept down.

I heard a scraping sound to my right, a quick, low voice said, "Roamer!"

It was Jack.

"You shut up!" That was Delacroix. The man was on the full boil once more.

I heard more scraping, a muffled sliding sound, somebody was moving through snow, then Jack's voice shouted, "You got no place to go, Delacroix!"

The killer's voice rose even higher, reached its peak, cracked, and then the gun barked once more—a bullish flash of light, like a quick campfire in midair, then near-dark once more.

"Enough!" The girl's voice was close. Might be I'd passed behind her. She was alive, boisterous, bossy, even. But Jack was my concern.

"Where is that son of a bitch?" Delacroix forced his rage

through clenched teeth.

I guessed he was looking for Jack. So was I. He wasn't too far away, and from the sounds of it, was in full throat and riled as a bull calf in spring. I might be overstating his condition, but it was good to hear him coherent and close by.

My next step met with something soft. I pulled my boot back, bent low, and pawed the thing. As I did this, I heard Delacroix cursing, saying, "Come on, come on!" then scratching sounds.

The thing I'd been pawing pawed me back, punching at me, if I were to tell the truth. "Boy, keep those big mitts to yourself!"

Jack.

I bent low, still pawing, and found what I suspected was his head. "Jack?" I whispered. "That you?"

"Who in the hell else you think'd be out here, chewing snow and arguing with crazy folk?"

The scraping I'd heard was Jack dragging himself off a boulder and plowing snow on knee and elbow to get behind the rock. A big risk, but he'd been certain I was there. Glad I was.

That's when the matches Delacroix had been scratching finally took hold. The brief flare illuminated enough to show me where he stood. I rose up on one knee, but the light dropped down, not out, hidden again from me. Then, against all possibility in that raw spot, blacker than a bull's backside, as Jack says, the night lit bright.

I risked rising up on one knee again and saw a whole lot at once: The light bloomed outward in all directions from an oil lantern with a wire bail atop, gripped in one hand by the killer.

With the brightness rose the cackling laughter of that madman. "I see you now!"

The night grew even brighter for one match-flare moment as two guns burst their intentions in spark, flame, and smoke.

I shot at the same time Delacroix did. His bullet buzzed my head too close, closer than any bullet had come without leaving its mark on me. Mine didn't come as close to him as that, but it did shatter the lantern's glass globe.

I saw it all happen as if time had slowed for that brief moment—the glass burst, the killer's hand jerked, his fingers spasming rigid. His leering laugh became a scream as his head whipped backward. I heard another shout, then, had to be the girl. I hoped she hadn't been hit somehow.

I was set to bolt forward when I felt a hand grip my boot. Jack. Maybe the bullet had gotten him? I dropped low.

"Jack, you okay?"

"Yes, but you got to know something, boy . . ."

"No time," I said, rising. "Got to get the girl while I can!"

"Roamer!" He shouted and tried to grab my boot again but I stepped away, keeping low. In the dark once more, I angled around the boulder, listening for the killer's howls and moans, but they'd pinched off.

I hoped he was incapacitated enough that I could get the girl out of there and then lash Delacroix up tighter than a water-soaked hat.

Ahead, I heard a flurry of words rip through the air. "I'll kill the bastard! I will!" Then a slap—a hand on a cheek? More whispers, shushing sounds, a scuffling, scraping, maybe feet in the snow. The sounds trailed away, downslope to the north.

I inched closer to where I thought she'd stood. "Girl? Annette?" I half-whispered the words. "Follow my voice, get on out of here now!"

Nothing. No noise, nothing. Then I heard soft thudding sounds below, downslope, too far to chase in the dark, blowing night.

Something came up behind me. "Boy, they're gone again. Went down to where he left the horses."

"Dammit!" I said, then quiet as we stood side by side in the storm. Soon enough all I heard was the wind keening through the branches and my own breaths working my chest like a bellows.

"I have to go after them," I said, turning to Jack.

"Slow down, they can't get far in this mess."

"I reckon." I fumbled for his hands. "You still tied?"

"No, I'm a beaver, gnawed my way through these wrappings. What do you think, you whelp?"

I smiled, despite the situation. "Good to see you, Jack." I wrapped him in a big bear hug. He hates that sort of thing. And I imagine not being able to push me away with his tied-up mitts made it even worse.

"Leave offa me, you brute, and slice through these straps!"

We leaned against the rock for a few minutes, letting Jack rub his wrists and shake his hands to get the blood flowing again. I was anxious to follow Delacroix and the girl, but Jack was right. With any luck, for her sake, they would be holed up somewhere out of the wind.

"How's your head?" I said, turning to him. I saw his outline through the snow.

"Better now that you squashed me."

I smiled, and said nothing. In a few moments he said, "I reckon I'll live. Been through worse."

"That Delacroix, he's a piece of work, ain't he?" I said.

"Roamer, you recall that tale I told you?"

"You talk a lot, Jack. Care to narrow down your thinking?"

"You ungrateful . . . the one about the goose that laid the golden eggs!"

I nodded, then a sudden thought I did not like at all hinted at where Jack's words were leading.

"Well, she's his goose," he said, and looked at me.

I shook my head no.

He nodded and continued. "And he's the greedy son of a bitch."

I kept shaking my head, not wanting to hear this, more convinced of anything in my entire scar-pocked life that he was wrong. Jack ignored me.

"Let's hope he doesn't kill his goose." He sighed, raised his eyes, and looked at me. "Roamer. I ever lied to you?"

I had to shake my head no. Didn't want to, but it was the truth. Jack's a whole lot of things, including a stretcher of the truth when it suits him, but he's no liar, which to my mind, is a whole other breed of cat than a teller of windies.

"I've spent a fair amount of time in their company, those two, and I know lovebirds when I see them. Stunty, freakish birds, but love comes in all flavors and shapes, boy." He looked at me in that way Maple Jack has. Those old blue-gray eyes sharp and clear as spring-melt ice, or they would have been had it not been so dark. "I know how it can be, son. The heart is a horse with blinders on."

My jaws ground together hard, so hard I thought for certain my back teeth would powder. But they didn't. I worked through all the usual tensed muscle, neck-aching moments, and eventually, after a full minute or two of staring him down and not gaining any sort of foothold on the rocky crag that is Mount Maple Jack, I sagged. My big shoulders drooped and I nodded. "Okay, I guess somehow I knew as much."

He said nothing but clapped a grimy old hand on my shoulder and squeezed once. "Good. I'm about talked out. Let's catch us a greedy son of a bitch. And . . ." he winked, I think. "Rescue a golden goose." He indicated I should lead the way.

I stumble-footed the short distance back to Tiny and Mossy, still tied in the trees downslope.

Jack made straight for his mule, who was all perky ears and nodding head. Over his shoulder, Jack said, "And for heaven's sake, take off my fur topper before that big heathen head of yours stretches it all out of proportion!"

Jack.

I smiled.

Chapter Twenty-Five

Turns out Jack was right. There was no way they were going anywhere that night. Same with us, though we tried. But the storm grew bolder, the wind howling and whipping snow into a blinding mass. The sounds raking and rattling the trees kept us all on edge. Tiny Boy and Ol' Mossback, tired as they were, stood jitter-eyed and with nostrils flexed.

I moved them to a less breezy spot in a copse, partially ringed with boulders. I tied them well, and fed and watered them. It wouldn't do to be afoot come the morning.

Jack waved away my efforts at helping him, so I built a fire pit and scooped out a snug bowl around it, mounding snow high to keep the wind from dancing our fire. I layered it with spruce boughs. It would make a decent place to hunker and sit out the storm, loathe as I was to do that, knowing the killer and the girl were out there in the dark. Likely they were not all that far away, somewhere to our north, along the more exposed slopes of this rocky range.

While Jack rummaged in his goods, donned warmer gear, and grumbled a whole lot, I set to work heating a jar of Jack's precious whistle berries. I sliced in a few curls of fatback and set the coffee pot to boil. Jack appeared wearing his full-bore winter fur hat, the one with earflaps and a chin strap. It had gotten mashed in his bag and the lynx's face on the front of it looked more perturbed than usual to be sitting on Jack's knobby head.

Jack held aloft a corked bottle of near-clear liquid. "For the trauma, you see." He winked and poured a generous dollop into my cup, then his. The coffee was not yet boiling, so we sipped the fiery liquid straight.

There is nothing in the world so brutal and then so soothing as the trail moonshine leaves down a man's gullet. We both smacked our lips in pleasure at that first—always the best—sip.

"I see you found your winter hat," I said, nodding toward his head.

"Yep. You might as well keep that one. Stretched it all to hell. It'll never fit another human after snugging your pate."

"Why, thank you, Jack."

He turned away, kicking at his blanket. "Don't get teary on me. I was fixing to give it to you anyway. Happy Christmas early."

"Again, my thanks. You know, I had a fine pair of knitted red socks for you for Christmas, but . . ." I shrugged.

"Those rags you was wearing on your big paws when I saved your hide a few days back?" He snorted. "Keep 'em. You already wore the goodness right out of them. I'll expect something even fancier come Christmastime!"

"You got it." Happy as I was to have him safe and sound, I'd promise him most anything. Heck, maybe I'd lay in his entire store of firewood for the coming year.

Jack does like that holiday. I'd grown to look forward to it as well. It was a number of years ago on Christmas Eve, in fact, that he saved my life for the first time. But that's a story for another day.

I bent down and stirred the beans. They smelled sweet and peppery—time to eat. I dished them up and passed Jack a bowl-ful.

Over the rim of my own bowl, in the wavering orange light of the fire, I took a long peek at Maple Jack. He looked like he'd been dragged through a fiery creek in the lowlands of hell. My face must have showed what I saw.

"That bad, huh?" he said, tenderly touching the side of his head close to where he'd been clubbed.

"No, no, it's the light playing tricks. You don't look much different than usual." As soon as I said it I regretted it.

"Oh really?" He set down his tin bowl, still half-filled with hot beans, and two of his gut-buster biscuits wedged, softening, in the juices. "So you are saying I am normally a bloodied, befouled, ragged, mud-smeared mess with a limp and a sore chest . . . on both sides!"

I spooned in another mouthful of beans and shrugged, trying to hide a grin behind my bowl. "Well, you do limp much of the time."

He squinted at me, then dragged a grimy finger under his nose and smoothed his bedraggled moustaches. "You got me there." He picked up his bowl and blew on the beans. "I ever tell you how I got that limp?"

Now I'd heard a variety of variations on that very topic over the years, but I wasn't about to interrupt the man. He was back, and if he wanted to sing opera, I'd perk my ears to the task, unpleasant though it would be.

Later, after he'd finished with the story of how he earned his limp, a version I'd not been familiar with, we sat with cups of hot coffee. The tin mugs threatened to raise blisters on our hands, but it felt grand. Our footsoles steamed before the small campfire, our mittens and gloves doing the same, propped on leaning sticks and looking as if they were arguing in silence over which way to point.

I sipped, savoring the hot, bitter brew. "You think Delacroix will try to find us tonight?"

As if in answer, a gust whirled a cloud of snow crystals

overhead. Some drifted down, like magic dust in a child's fairy story.

Jack shook his head, then shrugged. "I was about to say no. But that rascal is a hard man to figure. I'll wager he has a death in his thoughts for you. You know," Jack squinted skyward. "There's a killer in all of us. Hell, that's not much of a revelation. Thing is, even the pinkest-palmed among us would agree if you get yourself backed into a corner, haired up and hissing, you'll defend yourself."

Jack sipped, then resumed speaking: "Shooting his lantern and peppering his face like that." He whistled. "He's vain, is that one. You likely scarred him up for life."

"With any luck, his life won't last all that long."

"Be a blessing," said Jack. "If ever there was a critter that earned a slow, painful death, it's Delacroix. But that don't mean we should be the ones to dole it out to him. Not unless he brings up the topic first, that is."

I chewed my lip, then nodded. "Yeah, you're right, I know." I ran my tongue over my teeth. "You think the girl's in danger?"

Again, Jack squinted in thought, sipping his coffee. Finally he said, "Naw, those two have something strange going on betwixt them. I overheard as much as I could, me being the curious sort. Also I was strapped to that saddle like a half a pig, jouncing along not two feet from them most of the time."

"But she sort of fell for him on the trail, right?" I looked at Jack, wishing he'd tell me what I wanted to hear.

He sipped again. "Near as I can figure, boy, they have known each other for some time. There was a whole lot of whispering, little looks my way as if they didn't dare say much in front of me. Why he didn't kill me, I'll never figure out, given the heathen he is." Jack sipped, snapped a finger, and said, "Now that I think on it, they each made mention at different times of a father. Hers, I think."

"Father?" I said, shaking my head. "No, that can't be right. Her aunt back at the train told me the girl was orphaned. Said the girl's father died in some horrible accident . . ." My words dribbled to a stop. I traded a look with Jack.

"Well now," he said, reaching for his rifle and draping it over his lap. "Much as I'd like to believe nobody's fool enough to venture from his camp on a night like this, that man's crazy as a hatful of bedbugs. We should take turns on guard duty."

I smiled. "I'll take the first watch, Jack. Get some sleep."

He hunkered down, pulled his Hudson's Bay blanket up under his chin, tugged his fur hat over his face, and said, "Wake me in a couple of hours. I'm like a mountain cat, don't need much . . . shut-eye . . ."

I watched the old codger's blanket rise and fall with his deep-sleep breaths. I had no intention of waking him before morning. I couldn't sleep if I tried. I had a whole lot to think about, a whole lot to do, and precious little time to do it.

"I am sorry to have gotten you into this, Jack," I said in a whisper. But I was thankful to have him safe once more, somewhat whole and partially sound. Same as always.

I rose, and tugging my own fur hat down low and snugging my sheepskin-lined collar high, I turned my head to my right and squinted into the dark, hoping to see the faint distant flicker of a fire. All I saw was snow blowing in all directions against a black backdrop. All I heard was the moan and hiss of wind.

Where are you, Delacroix? And Annette, the girl in blue— what have you done?

I edged away from the little campsite and disappeared into the trees, crazy to leave the warmth of the fire, crazy enough to venture into the storm.

CHAPTER TWENTY-SIX

I left our camp with the intention of scouting Delacroix's location. The notion of standing still in the shadows, watching our warm fire crackle, while Jack snored away like an old boar grizz was not appealing. Especially given the wind's bluster and dropping temperature. I figured a quick foray wouldn't hurt. It would keep my blood pumping, keep me from freezing solid, and would make finding that skunk far easier come dawn.

All I had to look for was a flicker from their fire. Maybe if luck was with me, I'd sniff smoke. I couldn't count on the wind carrying smells or sounds to me. It was driving in from every direction at once. I'd not trudged twenty yards from our own fire when a quick gust pawed at my hat, threatened to knock it clean off my head. It's a heavy fur hat and my head's big and the hat's jammed down onto it tight.

You'd think that would be enough to keep it snug atop me. But no, that gust hit and the hat pinched up, wobbled, and if my right hand hadn't clapped down on it, I don't know how far that fur topper would have rolled.

The storm had delivered a whole lot of snow in three or four hours, and it made for slow progress. I have a sizable stride but high-stepping through that snow, drifted or otherwise, was fast wearing me out. I paused, my chest heaving. I tried to control my breathing, so it wouldn't seem so loud to me. Unless I stumbled right on top of Delacroix and the girl, I doubt they would hear me. But that's cold comfort when you're stalking a devil.

Even with a hand cupped to my ear, swiveling my head this way and that, I couldn't hear a damn thing other than the wind whooshing through the trees, buffeting against everything it came across, me included. I'd about given up my scouting mission when I thought I heard a horse. I'd gone too far for it to be Tiny and besides, his sounds, especially in a storm situation, were likely to be deeper, with more rumble, and a definite edge of annoyance to them. The horse does not like to be uncomfortable. Can't blame him for that.

No, this was from ahead—I'd caught luck with the wind from the north. I fancy I smelled horse, too, though that was as likely to be wishful thinking. No matter, I'd heard a horse somewhere.

I bent low, waited, but I heard no voices quieting the horse, saw no movement other than the willy-nilly wind-driven snowfall. I stood in the dark until my teeth began to clatter. I squinted hard to thaw the ice on my eyelashes, wiggled my lips and nose and decided I wasn't doing anyone any good. If Delacroix intended to do what I was fool enough to do and track us to our campsite, I should be there. Let him come to us. I'd deal with him once and for all.

If, on the other hand, he was somewhere not far away in the dark, perhaps near that worried horse, then he was likely making do with a cold camp. None of this bothered me save for one reason, one thought that kept me lingering, worried, and dithering: the girl.

I know what Jack said, and I know he wouldn't make up such a claim, but I'd seen her on the train. I always fancied I was a decent judge of folks, most often after getting a good long look at their faces, in particular their eyes. And that girl's eyes were like none I'd ever seen.

Was I smitten? I'd say so. I should have cared more than I

did about my blindness where the girl was concerned. Something about her kept me from thinking right. I sighed, shook my head like a wet dog, and lumbered on back to camp through the ever-deepening snow.

When I arrived after my foray, I looked at Jack—he hadn't moved, still snored in a deep slumber. I layered three snapped branches on the fire, then risked two minutes warming my hands and face and backside. No bullets sliced in from the dark and cut me low, so I took that as a sign that we were not yet in the gun sights of Mr. Henry Delacroix. But that didn't mean I was lulled into complacency by the hardship stormy weather brings.

I drizzled the last of the coffee into my cold, empty cup, sipped it down, then set the cup back at the melted edge of the pit fire. My big, cold fingers found two rock-hard biscuits and a frozen length of peppered jerky in my left saddlebag, flopped atop the mound of gear we'd made when we unburdened the grateful boys of their loads.

With my rifle in the crook of my arm, I made my way back into the trees on the south side slope of the campfire. Slow as a thought no one wants to think, I eased my way upslope so that if I had to tear back into camp I could do so with gravity and momentum on my side.

Confident I was hidden from spying eyes, I leaned against a pine and did my best to keep my eyes open. Unlike countless other nights on the trail, alone and with Jack, when I'd had reason to be suspicious of critters, two- and four-legged alike, on this night I found it easier to stay awake. I owed it to Jack, plus the snow and wind showed no sign of easing. That made it ideal for leaning and scanning, though there was precious little to see.

Hours later, through my dazed, snow-flurried gaze, I saw movement down by our now-dwindled campfire. I tugged off a leather mitten and rubbed my thumb and fingers into my eyes to melt the ice crystals there and on my rangy, whiskered face. The wind had eased.

The movement I saw was Jack. I think. I decided not to risk it, so I bent low, felt the pops and creaks and twinges of hot pain in my angry, bum knee, sore feet, stiffened back. I tried to catfoot on down closer to the fire pit and my mentor. I made it about twelve feet.

"That you, boy?"

I should have known. In my efforts to keep quiet I missed the snow-covered bulk of a boulder, and rammed that lumpy knee straight into an unforgiving face of the rock. It was my stifled groan that Jack heard.

"I've heard quieter banshees, you great oaf! Seein' as how you're up and about, stumble on down here and tend to this fire. I can't find my bottle."

Jack is not the most cheerful soul when he wakes. And on this early morning he wasn't about to alter that habit.

Maybe it was his jovial mood, or the fact that my body was a slab of iced meat, but I told myself to hell with it and I tossed any basket of caution I'd been carrying off into the snow as if it had been a foolish thing to cradle all night. I stumbled on down to the campsite.

I set one big, wet boot, then the other, at the melted rim of the fire pit and slid down the three feet. It felt good to sit. I did so for a full twenty seconds before Jack recommenced his predictable morning diatribe.

As tuckered out as I was, it was good to hear him, ranting and growling, cursing everything from his sore ribs to his still-damp moccasins. Then he found his corked bottle of "medicinal tincture" and he swigged, and smiled for the first time that day.

A bullet blew the bottle apart. Then another burned a sizzling, smoking furrow right between my left sleeve and my coat.

My old Schofield? Was there no sense of devotion, for old time's sake?

Jack and I both rolled down low beneath the rim of the fire pit. Only an arch of melting snow separated us from another bullet.

The old master of scrapes he is, Jack had snagged his rifle before he scrambled for cover. I still had mine gripped in my right, cold-clawed hand.

"Now he made me mad."

"Jack," I said. "That man has clubbed you, kicked you, kidnapped you, killed horses and men and lord knows who or what else, and we aren't done with him yet. And you're just now getting angry?"

Maple Jack eyeballed me, one brow high, the other crusted with dried blood set in a bruised, grimy, dirt-smeared face, and topped with a leaning fur hat with a mashed-in, ticked-off lynx glaring at me like a second head. "That son of a bitch shot my trail jug! My medicine, boy! I may not make it through! I'm so mad I could chew railroad track and spit nickels!"

I didn't have the heart to mention that tracks are steel. "What would you like to do, then, Jack?" He hates it when I pretend I'm calm in such a situation. Truth be told, a creeping wetness in my side told me that lucky shot that sliced between my sleeve and my coat might have been less-than-lucky for me.

"He's drawing us out, that alone should tell us what we need to do, boy." Jack was all business now, bent low and surveying the still-dark slope before us. "I don't think he's all that close, but I think the rascal's a good shot."

"Not good enough, or he would have killed us."

"Why would he miss us intentionally?"

I shrugged, looked upslope.

"Why toy with us? Why not toy with us? Hell, I ain't no philosophizer, all I know is that crazy man wants us dead. And we've all been sitting on our hands all night. Time to get on with it!" He winked at me. "Got things to do this winter, or have you forgotten?"

Even in the thick of it, Jack makes me laugh. I checked that my rifle was ready, then said, "You wait here, cover the horses. I'll drop back, head downslope, then north. With any luck we'll bookend him, pressure him from both sides."

Jack nodded. "Fine by me, but what about the girl?"

I looked away. "Worry about that when I find her."

"You aren't thinking right, Roamer. She's not what you want her to be. She's what she wants to be."

I kept low, backed away from the campsite. "Maybe, maybe not. But so far he's the one who's done all the killing." I didn't wait around for Jack to tell me I was being irrational about the girl, naïve, even. I knew it. And he did, too. To his credit he didn't say anything more.

"Don't risk your neck, Jack," I said, knowing that would leave him steaming.

I think the jasper retreated once he tossed those bullets at us, some odd way of letting us know he was still alive, and angrier than ever. But I wasn't so confident in my logic that I tossed away caution as I resumed my search for Delacroix, the human saddle burr.

The wound in my side, I knew from past experiences, hadn't driven into my body, but it had plowed a furrow in my flesh, I'll wager. I didn't want to take the time to look. I figured as long as I could still walk, breathe, and squint, I would survive to listen to Jack another day.

Within ten minutes, I came upon the spot they must have camped. It looked to have been a cold camp, and they'd huddled in the midst of what at first I took to be boulders. As I walked closer, my eyes skittering all about me, I saw they were not big rocks but three dead horses. That meant a fourth was somewhere—alive or dead, I knew not yet.

What had the man done? Killed his only means of escape? More likely he'd ridden them too hard, not tended them, and now they were useless to him. This was a man without the ability to sow seeds now in order to eat in the future. I noted, too, they appeared to still be loaded down with gear, saddles, bags, and all. What a sad mess.

Looking upslope, I saw a trail, scuffed wide enough in the snow that it could have been made by two people. I stepped over the nearest horse, toed the depression in the center of the three snow-mounded bodies, and found no coals, no ashes, no sticks. What a night to have no warmth from a fire. My toe prodded up a wad of blankets. That's all they'd had to cover themselves with? Delacroix must be more afraid of us than I thought he'd be.

Something moved off to my left. It ducked down again behind a snowy berm, poked up once more. Something covered in fur. The fur rose higher and I saw the face of a lynx, then Jack's bushy brow beneath it. I gestured with a hand at the cold camp to indicate they weren't there, then pointed at the trail leading straight into the trees at the base of the slope.

Jack nodded and we advanced.

CHAPTER TWENTY-SEVEN

With Jack ambling like a slow but deadly prairie fire, and me closing in from the north, we moved Delacroix and the girl like cattle, right where we wanted them to go. And that turned out to be nowhere at all. We'd cornered him tight into what might qualify as the smallest box canyon on a map. It was little more than a wedged cleft of sheer rock, steep, scree-riddled slopes leading upward to its dead corner. Light snow continued to fall from a gray morning sky.

We'd closed ranks, Jack to my left, me north of him. We held our ground, about forty feet apart, I was crouched behind tumbledown boulders, Jack behind a boulder and a snag of dead tree, what wasn't caked with snow was silvered and dried with age.

We both held a rifle trained upward at the clot of snow-covered trees maybe a hundred yards upslope, the last sizable spot for them to have holed up. Besides, their tracks led to it and didn't look to trail from it.

What was Delacroix thinking? That's the trouble with a madman, he gave up logical thought, I told myself. But that didn't mean he'd surrendered his ability to kill.

"Boy," Jack whisper-shouted to me. "We got to keep pressing. Remember she's his golden goose."

"Jack, that story didn't end well for the goose, if you recall."

"Oh, right, well . . . he won't harm her."

"What makes you so sure?"

"He's too greedy."

I didn't think Jack's logic was all that strong, but what else could we do? The next thing I knew, Jack fired a shot at the trees, but too high up to hit anyone. It did the trick.

As a cloud of blue smoke rose from Jack's rifle, Delacroix howled a single word: "Bastards!" Then he sent a volley of shots in our direction.

I had no idea how many bullets he had in his pockets, but if he kept lobbing them at us like that, he was bound to run out long before we did. For once, I had the upper hand in this wearying chase. It should have felt better. As if to pound the point deeper, the killer shouted, "Hey! Hey down there!"

"What?" I said.

"We're coming out, I still have the girl and if you try to shoot me, so help me this pretty little thing will not live another full minute of her life. You gonna wear that thought in your mind for all time, Big Boy? Huh?"

His voice had backed away from the frantic scream-edge of a few seconds before, though he was never far from it. Then I heard another voice, hers. I couldn't make out the words but the voice was sharp, hurried. His reply, too low to hear, was followed with a snapping sound like a breaking twig. Or a slapped cheek.

I took a deep breath. "Delacroix. . . ." I looked over at Jack, who didn't say a thing, but squinted at me through the light falling snow. It had begun to collect on his eyebrows, beard, and shoulders. He was here because of me. I did not want this to end badly. But how else could it?

The breeze had stopped some time before and I hadn't noticed. I was tired, bone tired, dog tired, plain tired of all this. Of the greedy people of the world getting anything they want without working for it. They stomp over the rest of the folks, the ones who want nothing more than to live quiet, happy lives, to smile at those they love and work a full day and get paid in kind for their hard efforts.

I wanted Jack to have the good season he'd planned with his winter woman, holed up with her at Salish Lake in Montana Territory. I wanted my bag of books, and then I wanted to go somewhere and be left alone to drink coffee and read and not be anywhere near people like Delacroix. But it seems the world is fast filling with people who want a whole lot without doing much for it. And at that moment high in the hills, I was tired of such folks.

The nearest was dead ahead of me. I knew what he was going to do next, and I was not inclined to give in to him any more.

"I am waiting, Big Boy!"

I scratched the tip of my nose. "Delacroix, Jack and I can wait here all day and all night. And the next after that!" I let my bellowed words echo around the dead-ended cleft. "But I doubt you can."

"I said I have the girl, Big Boy!"

He was nibbling on a crazy cracker again. I could hear it in the way his voice rose up high at the end, as if doubting himself.

"Yes, you do! Turn her loose and then we'll talk. Or you can both stay there." Again, my words echoed off the rock face above them. "All winter for all I care. I have nowhere else to be!"

I glanced at Jack. He whispered loud enough for me to hear. "I got somewhere to be, by god!"

I shook my head at him and turned back to the scene above.

"I don't think that's the way we are going to play this game, Big Boy! I am going to step out and if you so much as twitch in my direction, I will kill this pretty little thing! Oh, I know how you feel about her. I saw you on the train! You had that moon-face look, a big dumb bull in love!"

With no warning, Delacroix stepped out from behind the trees. True to his word he stood behind her, holding the girl, still wrapped in her blue cape. She appeared rough, her pretty face was shadowed with thinness and smudged with grime, her gold hair looked long-untended, strands blew about her face in the breeze, and her hands were wrapped in what looked to be dirty socks.

Delacroix didn't look much better. That starched collar had long since disappeared, leaving a grimy, stalky neck in its place. His confident face was thin, the left eye swollen but still open a crack. His cheeks gaunt and pocked on the left side with ugly blue and purple welts—remnants of the lantern's exploding glass globe.

His left arm encircled the girl, forcing her breasts and arms upward. Her mittened hands rested atop one other. It could almost have been a casual pose two lovers might hold. Except that in his right hand he held a sizable revolver, my Schofield. It prodded her forehead, the thin skin of her temple dimpling around it.

Her eyes only looked half afraid, though. As if she trusted that something good—or at least something she wanted—would soon come of all this. I half expected to see her mouth spread into a wide grin, but it was a forlorn slit between two thin, blue lips.

I did not know what to make of these people. But I didn't have long to think. A wide smile spread across Delacroix's face and he shouted, "We'll be climbing on down now. If either of you blinks I'm going to shoot this foul creature in the head!"

"No you ain't, neither," said Jack and rose from his crouch behind a boulder. "You two lovebirds got it all figured out, eh?" He cranked the lever on his rifle. "Going to mosey on down and ride off to your riches over in Seattle, was it?"

"What's wrong with having plans in life, old man? As for us

being lovebirds, I assure you, nothing is further from the truth. This trollop has been less fun than I expected. But as she is so very pretty, and I know Big Boy is smitten with her, he is bound to kick up a fuss should I spill her blood and brains all over this godawful snow." He cackled in that crazy way of his.

I could take no more of his foul words, and I, too, raised my rifle to my shoulder. "Shut it, Delacroix. No man has the right to speak of a lady in such a manner."

"Lady? Ha!"

"Oh, pish posh!" shouted Jack. "Too much palaver! Set the girl free, drop that gun, and raise your arms high!"

"Or you will do what, old man?"

"This," said Jack.

I should have known what was about to happen, as Jack is not one to stand around in the snow, chatting and frittering, when obvious action can be taken. I didn't even have time to shout Jack's name in warning. I needn't have worried, he shot straight and true, something I would not have dared at that distance.

His bullet did the trick, however close it came to the girl. Too close, in my opinion. But I couldn't argue with the results. Henry Delacroix screamed like he did when I'd shot the lantern in his face.

It was as if we were watching a conjuring trick in a stage show. One second, the killer held the girl in a tight grip, the revolver's deadly end rammed into her temple. The next second, Jack's rifle cracked and Delacroix's right leg whipped upward behind him as if jerked by a cosmic hand tugging a string. Blood sprayed a red rainbow across the glittering, snowed slope behind him.

The force of Jack's shot, which plowed straight and true into the meat of the killer's lower leg, pitched Delacroix onto his left elbow. The arm gave way and he flopped to his back. I watched my Schofield spin out of his hand, arc high ten feet, then disappear into the snow.

The killer landed hard, his shot leg pinned beneath him at an angle nature never intended. The girl spun from his grasp and stumbled downslope before pitching forward to her hands and knees as if she were a rag doll dropped from on high, her grime-smeared blue cloak vivid against the snow. But no rag doll could howl such as she did, matching Delacroix's screams of agony with her own, at once fearful and angry.

"No! No!" she shouted over and over, scrabbling to claw her way upslope to reach the writhing Delacroix.

Jack and I were both on the move, but we'd underestimated the girl. She made not for Delacroix but for the Schofield. In seconds she'd dragged her hands through the hole it had made in the snow and plucked up the gun.

She sat back and held the big pistol in both hands. I couldn't tell if it was cocked or not, but I regard any gun pointed in my general direction as a danger. Not much of a surprise, she pointed it downslope, first at Jack, then swung it toward me. She was three feet above the whimpering Delacroix.

Jack shouted, "Don't do it, girl!"

At the same time I said, "Ma'am, now don't you do that!"

She didn't seem to hear us. Her eyes were slitted, mouth pulled tighter than before, her nostrils gave away her hard breathing, flexing as if they couldn't draw enough air.

"Give me that gun!" Delacroix screeched, crabbing his right hand at her.

I had to give the man credit, he was in a welter of pain yet he had enough wit to keep demanding. And I gave her less credit than I thought she deserved—she scooted downslope, her long skirts bunching up around her backside so that her underskirts and longhandles showed above her black boots. And she handed him that gun, her jaw thrust outward in defiance, teeth gritted.

Not once did she take her eyes off the two of us, skittering them from Jack to me and back.

"No, I say!" Jack snugged his rifle tight to his shoulder. I didn't know who he was fixing to shoot next, but I suspected it wasn't the girl. Considering she was now unarmed, I expect he was keen to deliver another shot to Delacroix.

Then the girl shocked us again. She scrabbled her way downslope, and draped her body over Delacroix, legs spread wide, facing upward, doing her best to shield the killer from us. Delacroix groaned. I expect she jostled his shot leg. Good.

"You leave him alone!" shouted the girl. "Leave him be!"

"Girl, this don't make sense!" Jack shouted at her, but kept the rifle pinned on the two of them. "He is a murderer and a thief, and a killer of innocent horses, besides! You're too good for the likes of him!"

Jack's speechifying made no difference. She stayed spraddle-legged, her blue cloak outstretched. All I could see of the killer was his left boot and his left arm, wagging as if he was trying to conduct a string quartet. I heard him, though. The man was howling up a storm and soon enough he commenced to bouncing and bucking. The girl stayed atop him, though, swaying and jerking and doing her best to keep him hidden from view.

If I didn't know better, I'd have yelled to Jack to avert his eyes. As it was, when I glanced over at him, my mentor caught my eye and whistled, gave his head a slight shake. I'd hear about this later. Maple Jack is not one to let a ribald moment, real or imagined, pass without comment.

Delacroix was either in a full-bore rage or he was thrashing in agony. Maybe a bit of both. He shouted, "Get off me, damn you!" and flung the girl from atop him.

She flopped downslope, face-first in the snow, shouting, "No! No!" With the dedication of a prize hunting dog, she did her best to right herself and crawl back to his aid.

Delacroix had other intentions and he shouted them with all the wrath a wounded man with a bad case of anger can shout. "You dare shoot me? Corner me, a Delacroix of Savannah? Refuse to let me travel on my way? Gaah!"

That seized the girl up short. She glared at us, eyes narrowed and, on her mouth, the thinnest of smiles to match. It was as if she thought this might make all the difference to us.

Jack sucked hard through his nose, spit something wet and nasty-sounding. For theatrical effect, of course. It worked, all eyes looked his way. He never took his squinty eye off his rifle sights.

I piped in: "Seems to me you aren't alone in this Delacroix. Or perhaps you'd forgotten about her?"

The girl whipped her gaze at me, and I saw quick, wild eyes set in dark purple-black smudged hollows—why hadn't I noticed how animalistic she'd become? What happens to some among us on this long, lonely, rubble-strewn path of life that bends us in such a way? Makes us grab with both hands the very thing that wants to kill us most? Or worse, ignore us?

No matter if my guess was wrong or right, so help me, in that second, if she hadn't been smack between me and him, I'd have driven two bullets into his foul face. As it happened, as he has so many times in the past, Maple Jack took care of the situation for me.

While I'd shouted to Delacroix, and the girl turned her haggard beauty on me, Jack kept his rifle lined square on the killer. Good thing, too, as Delacroix had, in his ravings, spied Jack peering above the boulder. The killer howled like a man who'd bucked the tiger and won big. He raised that Schofield in a steady hand. I saw it level off behind the girl, who'd turned away from me.

She and I shouted the same word at the same time, though for different reasons: "No!"

Our twinned commands exploded with the bullish roar of two guns at once. I saw Delacroix's right arm buck with the Schofield's recoil, saw a cloud of blue smoke bloom, pollen gusting from a tainted flower, then turned as if time had slowed, to see Jack drop low behind the gray, snowy boulder.

"Jack!"

Time took its time. Eventually my old friend looked over at me, eyes narrowed beneath the leering angry face of the lynx. He nodded once. I knew then he was not hit.

But Henry Delacroix, of the Savannah Delacroixs, was. The girl caught on even sooner than I did. Her screams ripped from her, burst outward long and loud enough to touch off a snow-slide. But the slopes high above us were too steep to hold more than a trace.

The craggy edifice stood tall and bleak, echoing her pain back down on us like a storm raging in hell itself.

Jack and I dug our boots into the scree slope at the same time, scrabbling to reach her. But the girl in blue was high above us, and her grief was not yet that, but seething anger, confusion, doubt, perhaps hope. Her kisses and squeezing of his face could not rouse Henry Delacroix, he of the Savannah Delacroixs, from the deepest of slumbers. Jack's bullet had driven deep into the man's brain.

I was still twenty feet below her when she clawed up the Schofield once more, thumbed back the hammer, and screamed words without meaning to anyone but her. She raged at us even as her voice grew ragged, like shredded cloth in a driven wind. All the while she pushed backward up the slope, steep as it was.

Her right boot caught in a wedged gap between two rocks. She did not seem to notice, but jerked herself free and kept moving. The boot heel had torn free, the nail-stippled stack of black leather tumbled downslope, came to rest two feet above me. I don't know why this should matter, but it did. It does.

"No!" she shouted over and over, still scrambling upslope without looking.

Jack tried to talk to her all the while, tried to reason with her. Snatches of his words floated to me, ". . . going to be fine, girly . . . here to help you . . . nothing foolish, now . . ."

None of it, I knew, would matter to her. Hers was the worst torment of all, shame and grief and rage and desolation and confusion, all of it and more. And still it was not enough to fill her, would never be. For there is no consolation to a heart torn apart by violence.

She kept the Schofield wagging between the two of us. Jack held his rifle halfway raised, and walked forward, turned to the side, to make himself less of a target. I hated to tell him his belly made that impossible.

She reached a shelf of jutting stone, high enough for her to step up, her left hand clawing for knobs of rock sticking out. In her right hand, she held the weighty pistol in a shaky grip, which made the thing all the more menacing. One slip and her finger would touch off a stray bullet.

"No, Annette!" I finally shouted, "Stop this now! Your aunt is worried—she's waiting for you! We . . . we can make this right!"

She spat then, kept climbing, kept her eyes on Jack mostly, as if she knew he was the one she had most to fear. Finally she looked at me. "Right? Right? You big, filthy, ugly animal! You . . . you killer! You know nothing!"

The words stung, I will not deny it. But she was still there, alive before me. The allure of possible redemption is a mighty tempting tonic. I swallowed back her hate and climbed higher. So did she.

By then she had reached another shelf, narrow, of wet, black rock. She pulled herself up, and stood. It cracked, gave way beneath her, and she screamed.

Her right arm whipped high as her body dropped, bending

almost impossibly in the middle. The Schofield blasted skyward. The girl fell, blue cape flaring, worthy of a glorious stage production, the way it spread and fluttered, making sounds like the wings of a bird in spring, so happy for its good fortune.

She dropped the ten or twelve feet, and hit the slope hard on her right shoulder. Her legs flailed upward, forcing her to travel downslope fast.

Her wide, frightened eyes looked right into mine as I heard a noise that I will hope, to the end of my days, was one rock smacking another.

But I know that is not the truth. It was her pretty neck snapping.

The bird's wings folded, wrapping the long, slender body in grimy blue winding rags. She rolled, faster and faster, then came to a stop at my feet.

Her face stared upward, one eye open, one pretty blue eye, bloodied where before clear white surrounded an endless sapphire sea.

CHAPTER TWENTY-EIGHT

We found the last horse Delacroix had left alive. It was weak, but would do to carry the body of the girl, Annette, back to her aunt. The girl and the stolen goods, her inherited legacy, such as it was. I didn't look in the bags, but Jack did. Bank notes, deeds, bonds, various certificates.

Her father had been worth a fortune, and seemed to own half of Seattle's waterfront real estate. Jack suspected the girl and that southern devil had killed him for it. I choose to believe otherwise, somehow. Otherwise, lest I dwell on it too long, too deep, and think ill of her.

Jack peeled the shirt from my furrowed side and stoppered the fresh flow of blood. He bandaged me up without comment—one more wound, one more scar. Then he retrieved my old Schofield pistol from the snow. I told him to keep it. It'd be a damn long time before I set a hand on it. In my mind she was the last to hold it. Silly of me, maybe, but that's the way it is.

We stood for a long, long time at that spot, staring at the raw, windstripped slope. What foul mountain spirit had we offended here? Only the wind keening through the jagged gray rock dared intrude on our dire musings.

Finally, in a voice that surprised me with its quiet, shaky sound, I said, "What is this place called, Jack?"

It took him a couple of moments. He cleared his throat. "The Salish call it . . . the Valley of the Lost Lovers."

"Ah, I see," I said.

After a few more moments of silence, Jack said, "Roamer, son, you did more than anyone could. You—"

"No, Jack." I felt tears fill my big, foolish eyes. I shook my head. He is the only man I'd ever cried in front of. "I did this. I tailed them, I tracked them relentlessly through the snow, through that pass, dogging them without let-up. It was me all along. I killed the golden goose. Not him. She would be alive in Seattle right now. Happy and alive."

Jack grunted. "Not likely, boy. You think once he got her pappy's fortune he was going to put up with her? A firebrand like that?" He shook his head, a sneer pulling his mouth wide, as if he'd tasted something off. "No sir." Jack looked again at me. "You did what you had to do, what you knew was right, one and the same for a smart man."

I said nothing. I tried to listen to him.

"A dog goes bad," he said. "And it kills and kills and kills. Why, you have no choice but to return the favor. That son of a bitch," Jack thrust a big-knuckled finger toward the rough cairn we'd piled atop Delacroix's broken body. "He brought all this thunder down on his own head. No sir. You got no call to let this linger in your mind, picking away at you like a buzzard on a gut pile. You let it be. You got nothing to bear guilt over."

I heard every word he said, saw the truth tight on the lines of his old face, saw the weight of his words in his eyes. I have known the man a long time and never had he been more serious or earnest. But all I could picture was the girl's face, Annette, the girl in blue, smiling and wide-eyed and clean and pretty on the train.

Then, as quickly, that pretty face was replaced with the hollow-eyed, terrorized look she wore on the slope of that cursed mountain. And that image, in turn, was replaced with the last I would ever see of her face, bloodied and battered at my feet.

The winding sheet had covered her, but not in my mind,

never there. There she will roam alone, staring at me from within, never smiling, I fear, for the rest of my days.

I turned from Jack, turned from the mountain, held my homely face in my big, thick hands, and wept away the last of my heart.

"Oh, son . . ." said Maple Jack, resting a gnarled hand on my shoulder.

High above, the sky had begun to clear, promising a bright, blue day.

The end.

Roamer and Maple Jack will return.

ABOUT THE AUTHOR

Matthew P. Mayo is an award-winning author of more than thirty books and dozens of short stories. His novel, *Tucker's Reckoning,* won the Western Writers of America's Spur Award for Best Western Novel, and his short stories have been Spur Award and Peacemaker Award finalists. His many novels include *Stranded; North of Forsaken; The Outfit* series; *Winters' War; Wrong Town; Hot Lead, Cold Heart; The Hunted; Shotgun Charlie,* and others.

Matthew's numerous nonfiction books include the bestselling *Cowboys, Mountain Men & Grizzly Bears; Haunted Old West; Jerks in New England History;* and *Hornswogglers, Fourflushers & Snake-Oil Salesmen.* He has been an on-screen expert for a popular BBC-TV series about lost treasure in the American West, and has had books optioned for film.

Matthew and his wife, photographer Jennifer Smith-Mayo, run Gritty Press (www.GrittyPress.com) and rove the byways of North America in search of hot coffee, tasty whiskey, and high adventure. For more information, drop by Matthew's Web site at www.MatthewMayo.com.

The employees of Five Star Publishing hope you have enjoyed this book.

Our Five Star novels explore little-known chapters from America's history, stories told from unique perspectives that will entertain a broad range of readers.

Other Five Star books are available at your local library, bookstore, all major book distributors, and directly from Five Star/Gale.

Connect with Five Star Publishing

Visit us on Facebook:
  https://www.facebook.com/FiveStarCengage

Email:
  FiveStar@cengage.com

For information about titles and placing orders:
  (800) 223-1244
  gale.orders@cengage.com

To share your comments, write to us:
  Five Star Publishing
  Attn: Publisher
  10 Water St., Suite 310
  Waterville, ME 04901